Volume II

by James Preller

SCHOLASTIC INC.

New York   Toronto   London   Auckland   Sydney
Mexico City   New Delhi   Hong Kong   Buenos Aires

Contents

A Jigsaw Jones Mystery #7: The Case of the Runaway Dog, ISBN 0-439-11426-8,
text copyright © 1999 by James Preller. Interior illustrations © 1999 by Scholastic Inc.

A Jigsaw Jones Mystery #8: The Case of the Great Sled Race, ISBN 0-439-11427-6,
text copyright © 2000 by James Preller. Interior illustrations © 2000 by Scholastic Inc.
Excerpts from Stone Fox by John Reynolds Gardiner © 1980.
Reprinted with permission of HarperCollins Children's Books.

A Jigsaw Jones Mystery #9: The Case of the Stinky Science Project, ISBN 0-439-11428-4,
text copyright © 2000 by James Preller. Interior illustrations © 2000 by Scholastic Inc.

A Jigsaw Jones Mystery #10: The Case of the Ghostwriter, ISBN 0-439-11429-2,
text copyright © 2000 by James Preller. Interior illustrations © 2000 by Scholastic Inc.

Cover illustration © 1999 by R. W. Alley

Book design by Dawn Adelman.

12 11 10 9 8 7 6 5 4 3 2 1   5 6 7 8 9 10/0

Printed in the U.S.A.   40

This edition created exclusively for Barnes & Noble, Inc.

2005 Barnes & Noble Books

ISBN 0-7607-9586-X

First compilation printing, August 2005

The Case of the
Runaway Dog

For Nicholas —
thanks for the great ideas!

Chapter One

Pilgrims and Turkeys

I sat in my tree-house office, doing a lot of nothing much.

But that's the life of a detective. It's not always a parade of glory. There are days when I just hang around the office, waiting for the next case to show up.

I slugged down another glass of grape juice and decided to call it a day. After a quick phone call to Ralphie Jordan, we headed to Lincoln Park with my dog, Rags. The sky was clear and blue. A couple of

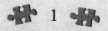

lonely clouds drifted by, looking like they were lost.

"Which is your favorite holiday?" Ralphie asked me as we walked into the park.

"Christmas," I answered.

Ralphie shrugged. "My family celebrates Kwanzaa, too."

"Do you get presents for Kwanzaa?"

"Sure," Ralphie replied. "But that's not what it's about. It's about celebrating our heritage."

I guess that was OK for Ralphie. Personally, I'd rather celebrate new toys. "How about this," I asked. "Which do you like better — Halloween or Valentine's Day?"

"Halloween," Ralphie answered. "More candy."

I agreed.

"How about Thanksgiving?" Ralphie asked.

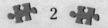 2

"I'm not crazy about the food," I complained.

"You know what bugs me about Thanksgiving?" Ralphie said, shaking his head. "Stuffing! I mean, what IS stuffing, anyway?"

"It's a mystery to me," I answered. "I'd rather have pizza any day." That settled it. When it came to holidays, Thanksgiving came in last place.

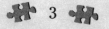

We stood in an open field. There was a big playground to our right. To our left was Long Hill — a big hill where we went sledding in the winter. And behind it was the lake.

Ralphie kicked a rock. "I have an idea," he said. "Let's pretend it's the first Thanksgiving. I'll be a Native American. You'll be a Pilgrim. And Rags can be the turkey!"

Rags looked up at us, alarmed. He didn't seem thrilled with the idea of playing a turkey. I couldn't blame him. After all, turkeys probably hate Thanksgiving. It's not exactly a terrific holiday when people eat you.

I let Rags off his leash. He was a good dog, in a slobbering kind of way. As usual, a string of drool dangled from his mouth. We pretended that our sticks were hatchets and chased Rags around the great lawn.

Suddenly, we saw Lucy Hiller, Mila Yeh, and Kim Lewis race past on Rollerblades. *Crash — kapowee!* They had a giant smack-up. All three of them were tangled in a knot. Ralphie and I raced over to make sure they were OK.

The girls were laughing like crazy hyenas. It was a good thing they wore helmets and pads. No one got hurt. After we talked for a while, I looked around and asked, "Hey, anybody see Rags?"

Chapter Two

The Search for Rags

"Here, Ragsy! Here, boy!"

"He's probably chasing a squirrel or something," Lucy offered. "My dog does it all the time."

I shook my head. "The only thing Rags chases is a free meal."

Ralphie frowned. "Maybe we shouldn't have been chasing him with sticks."

I put my hands to my mouth and bellowed, "Rags, come!"

Nothing.

Mila patted me on the back. She was my partner and best friend. "Don't worry, Jigsaw. He has to be around here someplace."

"What kind of dog is he again?" Kim asked.

"A Newfoundland," I said. "Gray and white. Just a big, hairy dog."

"Does he have a collar?"

"Yes," I answered. "And dog tags, too." That was the good news. If somebody found Rags, they could read our phone number and address on his tags.

We split up. Ralphie and I climbed the hill to search the trees. The girls did a loop around the park. On top of the hill, Ralphie and I could see in all directions. We saw a few people, but no dogs. "This isn't like Rags," I told Ralphie. "He'll wander sometimes. But Rags always comes back."

I pointed down toward the lake. "Let's see if anyone down there has seen him."

We talked to a man who was fishing from a rock. He hadn't seen anything. We talked to a lady with a baby. They were throwing bread into the water, feeding the ducks. They hadn't seen Rags, either.

"Maybe he wandered home," Ralphie suggested.

"That's across two streets!" I exclaimed. "Rags isn't allowed to cross the street by himself."

Now I was getting nervous. What if Rags *did* wander off? What if he got hit by a car? What if he . . . just . . . ran away?

"Rags!" I called out desperately. "Come on, boy!"

Ralphie pointed to a group of teenagers. "Hey, I know that girl. She lives across the street from me. That's Earl Bartholemew's sister, Carrie."

The teenagers were hanging out at the

edge of the lake. And they were doing what teenagers do best — just standing around, trying to look cool. Oh brother.

A girl with short black hair and a green jacket nodded hello. It was Carrie Bartholemew. "Hi there, Ralphie," she said, pushing him playfully. "Beautiful day, isn't it?"

"It used to be," Ralphie said, "until Jigsaw lost his dog."

Carrie looked at me and frowned. Carrie told us she hadn't seen any stray dogs. "We just got here," she explained.

Suddenly, Lucy Hiller, curly hair flying in the wind, called to us from the bicycle path.

"Jigsaw, come quick. Mila needs you."

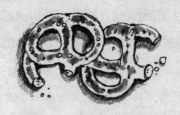

Chapter Three

A Strange Witness

There's a boathouse at one end of the lake. In the summer, people go there to rent paddleboats. Then they set out on the lake — for an afternoon of sunburn and mosquito bites. Go figure.

The boathouse was closed for the fall. It would open again once sledding season began. That's because they made a fortune selling hot chocolate to frozen kids. Next to the boathouse, there was a garbage Dumpster. That's where we found Mila and Kim, standing awkwardly on Rollerblades.

They were talking to an old man dressed in an overcoat. He wore a scarf and a cap pulled tight over his head. He had an enormous nose that reminded me of a bird's beak. The man squinted at us.

"Jigsaw, this is Mr. Signorelli," Mila said. "He says he saw a dog that might have been Rags."

The old man reached out a yellowed hand and I shook it. "Pleased to meet you." His grip was surprisingly strong. He pulled

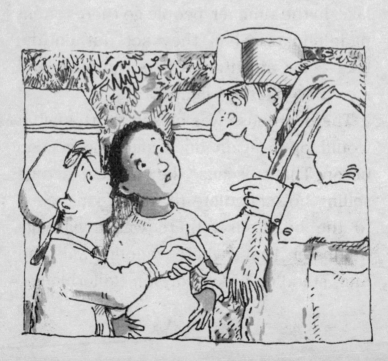

out a cigarette and lit it, coughing almost immediately. "I was just telling these young ladies that I did see something. Maybe it was your dog. Maybe not. My eyes ain't what they used to be."

Yeesh. A witness with bad eyes is like a polar bear wearing a purple tutu. Detectives don't have much use for them.

"I guess you could say this is my home away from home," he began. "Now that I'm retired, I spend most of my days in the park. I've made friends with a few squirrels. I bring 'em peanuts and we keep each other company. I don't know who looks forward to our visits more — me or them."

Mr. Signorelli took another deep drag of his cigarette. His eyes were red around the edges. And I noticed, for the first time, wisps of gray hair growing out of his ears.

"The dog," I reminded him. "You said you saw a dog."

"Pretty big one, too," he said. "Sniffing around by the Dumpster."

"Was he gray and white?" I asked.

Mr. Signorelli ran his fingers across his chin. A long, gray ash fell from his cigarette. "Maybe yes. Maybe no. With these eyes, I couldn't be sure one way or the other. But it was a big dog, I'll tell you that."

Mila coughed. "Mr. Signorelli, sir," she said. "Please tell him about the girl."

I shot a glance at Mila. "What girl?" I asked.

"Well, I *think* it was a girl," Mr. Signorelli said. "Hard to tell these days, ain't it? Boys wearing long hair and earrings and all. I can't keep track." He chuckled softly to himself. "Anyway, she was petting the dog. They seemed to be getting along pretty good."

"Did you notice anything else?" I asked.

Mr. Signorelli closed his eyes. For a minute, I almost thought he had fallen asleep. But he opened them suddenly and smiled.

"Pretzels," he said. "She was feeding him pretzels."

Chapter Four

Home Alone

When the sunlight touched the trees in the distance, I knew it was time to face my parents. They were going to kill me. The surprising thing was, I didn't even care. There was nothing they could say or do that would make me feel any worse.

We left the park empty-handed.

Lucy and Kim went home in the other direction. Heels dragging, I trudged between Ralphie and Mila. We stopped in front of Ralphie's house. "You okay?" he asked me.

I shook my head. "Nope."

Ralphie opened his mouth to speak. Maybe it was a joke or something to make me feel better. That would have been Ralphie's style. But he stopped short, turned, and ran inside the house. I guess he knew there was nothing to say.

Mila said good-bye, too. But I wasn't listening. All I could think about was Rags. He was out there somewhere. Maybe he was lost. Maybe he was hurt. I didn't know. I only knew that he was alone.

My family was already seated at the dinner table when I got home. "Where have you been?" my mother scolded.

But when she saw my face, her expression changed. "Theodore?" she said. "What is it?"

My father got up and walked toward me. "Son, are you all right? Where's Rags?"

It would have been easier if they yelled and screamed. But they didn't. My parents hugged me . . . and we talked . . . and they said everything was going to be all right.

"It's not your fault," my dad said. "It'll be okay. We'll find Ragsy, don't you worry."

My father threw on his coat and took my three brothers — Billy, Daniel, and Nicholas — in the station wagon. They went looking for Rags. My sister, Hillary, volunteered to call the animal hospital.

I felt a twinge in my stomach. "Animal hospital?" I asked.

My mother gave Hillary a look. "Just in case," my mother said. "I'm sure Rags is fine."

My mom tried to make me eat some macaroni and cheese. I took a few bites, but my heart wasn't in it. I went into my room and pulled out my detective journal. On a clean page I wrote: **THE CASE OF THE RUNAWAY DOG**. Usually, I loved mysteries. But that was when they happened to *other* people. This was *my* mystery — and it

wasn't any fun. I pulled out a jigsaw puzzle. It was a picture of cavemen battling a saber-toothed tiger. I gave up after a few minutes. None of the pieces seemed to fit. Finally, I crawled into bed and pulled the covers over my head.

Later, my father came home with my brothers. I could tell by their quiet voices that they'd come home alone. I rolled over in my empty bed. Rags was gone.

And it was all my fault.

Chapter Five

Room 201

On Monday, I wanted to stay home to help look for Rags. But my mother wouldn't listen. "You worry about school," she told me. "Rags will turn up."

"But . . ."

"But me no buts, Theodore," she said.

"But . . ."

Then she gave me . . . the look.

It meant: *End of discussion.*

Yeesh.

Mila sat next to me on the school bus.

Mila was usually singing a song, but not today. She was too busy thinking.

"What did you think of Mr. Signorelli?" she asked.

"I don't know," I answered. "He was kind of weird."

Mila shook her head. "Not weird," she said. "Lonely. There's a difference."

I thought about Mr. Signorelli. He did seem a little lonely, now that Mila mentioned it. He said the squirrels kept

him company. That's pretty bad, when squirrels are your pals. Maybe that's why he was so eager to talk with us. Mr. Signorelli didn't have anyone else.

"I'm too upset. I can't think straight," I told Mila.

"It's OK, Jigsaw," Mila said. "I'll help you find Rags."

Our class was in Room 201. We were lucky to have Ms. Gleason for a teacher. But I wasn't feeling very lucky. Or very thankful — which was too bad, since that was the topic of our homework assignment.

"Boys and girls," Ms. Gleason said, "Thanksgiving is in three days. You all know what that means."

Ralphie Jordan piped up, "Yeah, no school!"

Everybody cheered.

Ms. Gleason smiled. "Yes, we could all use a few days off." Then she told us about the first Thanksgiving. "Why were the Pilgrims thankful?" she asked.

"Because of the good harvest," Athena Lorenzo answered.

"That's right, Athena," Ms. Gleason said. "The pilgrims knew they had enough food for the long, hard winter ahead. They were thankful, so they had a big feast to celebrate."

Ms. Gleason stopped and looked at us. "Things are different today. We have supermarkets and restaurants and frozen TV dinners. Most of us aren't farmers. Why do we celebrate Thanksgiving now?"

No one had an answer. Mila slowly raised her hand. "To give thanks?" she asked.

Ms. Gleason smiled. "Yes, Mila. It's a day when we all give thanks."

Ms. Gleason wrote on the blackboard:

I AM THANKFUL FOR . . .

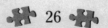

She continued, "On Wednesday, I'd like you to come in with a list of five things you are thankful for."

Bigs Maloney pumped his fist in the air. "Professional wrestling!"

"Sony PlayStation!" Eddie Becker called out.

Danika Starling protested, "You guys are all wrong. We're supposed to be thankful for important stuff." She cleared her throat. "I am thankful for . . . Beanie Babies!" Danika took a deep bow.

"That's very funny, Danika," Ms. Gleason said. "But there are no right or wrong answers to this homework assignment. The important thing is that you spend time thinking about it."

A few other kids spoke up. It seemed like everybody was thankful for something. But when Ms. Gleason called on me, my mind went blank. I couldn't think of anything.

Anything, that is, except for Rags. "I'm not feeling very thankful today," I mumbled.

Ms. Gleason made a face.

"Think harder," she told me. "We all have reasons to be thankful."

Oh brother. That was easy for Ms. Gleason to say.

Her dog wasn't missing.

Chapter Six
The Animal Rescue Shelter

Mila handed me a note at the end of the day. It was in code. She liked to test my brainpower. This time, she almost had me stumped.

24 * 11 33 * 22 35 24 34 22 * 12 11 13 31 * 45 35
* 32 35 35 31 * 21 35 43 * 33 35 43 15
* 13 32 51 15 44.

Then I remembered. It was called a checkerboard code. I pulled out my detective journal. First I drew a square with

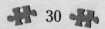 30

twenty-five boxes. Then I filled in the letters and numbered the rows and columns like this:

Column	1	2	3	4	5
Row 1	A	B	C	D	E
Row 2	F	G	H	I	J
Row 3	K	L	M	N	O
Row 4	P	Q	R	S	T
Row 5	U	V	W	X	Y/Z

To make the code, Mila changed each letter into a two-figure number. To make the letter *I*, for example, Mila wrote 24. The 2 stands for row 2. The 4 means column number 4. In another minute, I figured out the message. *I am going back to look for more clues.*

I looked up to see Mila smiling at me. I slid a finger across my nose. That was our secret signal. It meant I got the message.

When the bus dropped me off from school, the house was strangely quiet. No barks from behind the door. No happy dog jumping up to lick me. I usually hated it when Rags drooled on me. But today I would have given anything for a faceful of slime.

"Leave your coat on, detective," my oldest brother, Billy, called out. He came into the living room, twirling car keys around his finger. "We're going for a ride."

We drove steadily for about fifteen minutes. Billy pointed to a sign. "This is the place," he said.

The sign read: ANIMAL RESCUE SHELTER.

Billy winked. "You never know. We just might get lucky."

I'd never been to an animal shelter before. A very pretty girl with a long blond ponytail sat behind the counter. She had blue eyes and an earring in her nose. "Can I help you?" she asked.

"We're looking for our dog," Billy explained. "He disappeared yesterday and we were wondering . . ."

"The dogs and cats are through that door," the girl said. "We get a few new animals every day. Feel free to take a look."

In the next room, the walls were lined with cages, stacked three high. There was a cat in nearly every cage. Some were calm and beautiful; others were skinny and skittish. But they all shared something in common. They didn't have a home.

The dogs were kept in another room. It was like a big garage, with a cement floor and cement walls. The dogs were locked behind high, narrow fences. Some dogs sat and stared as we walked past. A cute Dalmatian leaped against the fence, whining sadly. Most dogs barked. You didn't have to be Doctor Dolittle to

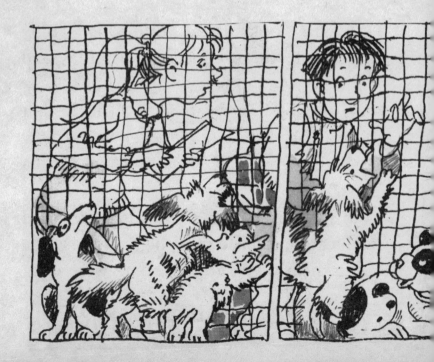

understand what they were saying —
"Take me, take me. I'll be good. Take me!"

Other dogs just lay on the ground beside their water bowls. They didn't seem to care one way or the other. They only lifted their heads and followed us with blank eyes.

It was one of the saddest places I'd ever been.

We didn't find Rags.

"Let's cut out of here," Billy said. "This place creeps me out."

On the way out, I asked the girl, "What happens to them?"

Her lips drew together tightly. "We never put them to sleep, if that's what you mean. This is a no-kill shelter. We hold on to our animals until someone adopts them."

"But what if no one . . . ?"

She looked steadily into my eyes. "We try to love them the best we can."

Billy dropped a handful of change into a donation box. "Thanks," he said. "You guys do good work."

And we left — the sound of barking still in our ears.

Chapter Seven

A Visit from Mila

There was a sharp knock on my bedroom door. Grams walked into my room before I could answer. I was lying on my bed, staring at the ceiling.

Grams turned on a lamp and opened the curtains. "It's too dark in here," she complained. "Why are you moping around, anyway?"

I sighed. Grams didn't understand. "There's no law against moping," I said.

"Around me there is," she snapped. "How are we going to get Rags back with

you lying in a dark room, feeling sorry for yourself? Come on, up and at 'em. We've got work to do."

She turned to leave the room. "And bring your markers," she demanded.

At the dining room table, Grams watched over my shoulder as I took out a large piece of paper. At the top, in big letters, I wrote the word MISSING! Below I drew a picture of Rags. "Looks just like him," Grams said approvingly. "Don't forget to include our phone number. I'll send your father to get copies made at Kinko's. It will be *your* job to put them up after school tomorrow."

I didn't hear the doorbell ring. That's because I was used to Rags. He was better than a doorbell, because he barked loudly when anyone came to the door.

"Your friends are here," my mom announced.

Mila came into the room. Kim Lewis, Lucy Hiller, and Ralphie Jordan followed.

"We went back to the park after school," Mila said. "We all wanted to help. Kim and Lucy found this."

Mila pulled a blue dog collar from her coat pocket. She handed it to me. I didn't need to read the dog tags. After all, I had picked it out myself.

"Where'd you find this?" I asked.

"Near the footbridge," Lucy answered.

"Maybe it came loose and fell off," Ralphie offered.

I didn't think so. The collar fit snugly on Rags. I checked to see if it was broken. The

collar snapped together easily. It was working just fine.

Mila pulled on her long black hair. "That leaves only one explanation," she said.

We all looked at her.

"Somebody took it off," Mila said.

She was right, of course. That was the only thing that could have happened.

Somebody took off his collar. But why?

I knew the answer immediately. But I didn't like it. Not one bit. They took off the collar because they didn't want Rags to be found.

He'd been dognapped.

Chapter Eight
The Green Thread

Something caught my eye. I looked closely at the collar. I carefully pulled off a green thread.

"What's that?" Kim asked.

I held the thread between my fingers. "This, my friends, is a clue. The dognapper may have been wearing green."

It was almost time for dinner. I walked my friends to the door. "See you, Jigsaw," Ralphie said.

As they started down the walk, I called

out to them. "Hey, guys," I said. "Listen, um, thanks — thanks a lot."

Grams was right. I was moping when I should have been hoping. Great detectives don't solve mysteries by lying around. They work. They examine clues. They visit the scene of the crime. They keep trying until the case is solved.

I ran to my bedroom and pulled out my journal. I listed the clues. Then I tried to think of suspects. I wrote down two:

Mr. Signorelli seemed nice enough. There was nothing about him that told me he was a dognapper. I remembered that his coat wasn't green. But the scarf . . .

It may have been green, or blue. I closed my eyes and tried to remember. What color was it? Could *he* have stolen Rags? Mr. Signorelli was lonely, I knew that much. He probably would have loved to have a dog to keep him company. I mean, a dog sure beats a lousy bunch of squirrels. Maybe he lied about seeing the girl.

I just couldn't be absolutely positive.

I telephoned Mila. She said Mr. Signorelli's scarf was red and yellow. "It couldn't have been Mr. Signorelli," she argued. "We saw him in the park when Rags disappeared. He was alone."

45

"Maybe," I said. "But anything is possible — and everyone's a suspect. I mean, how much do we *really* know about the guy? I'm going to have another chat with Mr. Signorelli tomorrow."

Mila paused on the phone. "I've been thinking about the girl with the pretzels," she said. "Rags likes pretzels, right?"

"Rags loves pretzels," I answered.

"Would Rags, maybe, follow someone . . . if they gave him pretzels?"

"He might," I said.

"We've got to find that girl," Mila concluded. "If Mr. Signorelli saw her in the park, maybe somebody else did, too."

"That's a big *if*," I replied. I reminded her that Mr. Signorelli's eyesight wasn't very good.

We reviewed the facts of the case. I told Mila about climbing the hill and going down to the lake. I told her about the man

on the rock and the mother and baby feeding bread to the ducks.

"Anything else?" Mila asked.

"Oh, yeah," I said. "There were some teenagers. One of them was Ralphie's neighbor, Carrie Bartholemew. But none of them saw anything."

"Were any of them wearing green?" Mila asked.

I pictured the teenagers in my mind. "Yes," I answered. "Carrie Bartholemew had short black hair . . . and a green wool jacket."

Chapter Nine
The Mystery Girl

I couldn't wait for school to end on Tuesday. "Remember your homework assignment," Ms. Gleason reminded us during cleanup. "I look forward to reading all the reasons why you feel thankful."

I eased over to her desk. "Excuse me, Ms. Gleason."

"Yes, Theodore?"

"Um, well, I can't do that assignment. Is there something else I can do instead?"

Ms. Gleason looked puzzled. "I don't understand," she said.

 49

I told her about Rags. "It's kind of hard to be thankful when you feel rotten," I explained.

"I'm sorry about Rags," Ms. Gleason said. "But you still have to do the homework. Even when we're sad, we all have reasons to be thankful. And when we're feeling rotten, it's especially important to remember the good things in life." Ms. Gleason shoved folders into her bulging book bag.

Without looking up, she said, "I expect to see that homework on my desk tomorrow, Theodore."

Yeesh.

We met in front of my house after school. Nearly everybody was there — Lucy, Kim, Ralphie, and Mila. I handed out posters and tape. We split up. The neighborhood would be plastered with posters in no time. But first, I handed Ralphie a baggy with the green thread. "I have a special job for you," I told him. "Somehow, you've got to get ahold of Carrie Bartholemew. Check this thread against her jacket. See if it's a match."

Ralphie looked at me, surprised. "Do you think she did it?"

"I don't think anything," I answered. "I just follow the clues."

I began to feel a little better. At least I was *doing something*, instead of moping.

I thought about what Ms. Gleason said. I guess you could say I was . . . *thankful.*

It was nice to have good friends.

Mila and I rode our bicycles into the park to look for Mr. Signorelli. We found him by the picnic tables, sitting alone, surrounded by a handful of squirrels. Mr. Signorelli held a peanut in his hand. Slowly, cautiously, a squirrel moved closer, closer. Suddenly, it snatched the nut and scampered away. You should have seen the smile on Mr. Signorelli's face.

"This is a nice surprise," he said as we pedaled to a stop. "I was just thinking about that dog of yours. Any luck?"

We shook our heads.

Mr. Signorelli pulled out a cigarette and began to light it.

"You shouldn't smoke," I said.

He scowled. "You sound like my doctor."

"No, just a friend," I replied. "Besides,

you don't need to be a doctor to know that smoking is bad for your health."

Mr. Signorelli sighed and laid the unlit cigarette on the picnic table. I handed him the poster. He eyed it carefully, holding the poster at arm's length. "That's the dog, all right. I'm sure of it."

He suddenly snapped his fingers. "You know, I just saw that girl a few minutes ago." He pointed toward the lake. "She was walking toward the footbridge. If you hurry, you can catch up with her."

We were gone faster than you can say Peter Piper picked a peck of pickled peppers.

We reached her before she crossed the footbridge. "Excuse me," Mila called out sweetly. "I was wondering if you could help us?"

The girl looked at us. "Oh, I suppose," she said reluctantly.

She was tall. Red sweater, jeans. Dirty blond bangs fell over her eyes. I figured her for ten years old. Eleven, tops. Probably a fourth-grader.

Mila gave her the poster. She glanced at it quickly, then shoved the paper into her jeans pocket. "I don't like dogs," she said.

"But have you *seen* him?" Mila asked. "We lost him in the park."

"Nope, never saw him in my life," she answered quickly. "Besides, I just moved here. And I definitely wasn't in the park on Sunday."

"Is that so?" Mila said.

The girl blew air out of her mouth, making her bangs rise, then fall. "I was at the mall all day, shopping. Any more questions?" She turned to leave.

I was about to speak when Mila poked me in the ribs. "Let her go," Mila whispered.

"But . . ."

Mila shushed me.

We watched her cross over the bridge and walk toward the street.

"Come on," Mila said. "Let's follow her."

Chapter Ten
Proof!

We hung back as far as we could, while still keeping an eye on the girl with bangs. She crossed the street, turned right, then walked up a stone pathway and disappeared into a yellow house. I wrote the address in my journal: 41 LAKEVIEW ROAD.

"She knows something," Mila said. "All we need now is proof."

I was surprised. "What makes you so sure?" I asked.

Mila nodded, grim and determined. "She made a mistake," Mila said. "She told us *too*

much. When people lie, sometimes they say more than they need to. Do you remember what she said when I told her we lost Rags?"

"She said she was at the mall all day," I answered.

Mila corrected me. "She also said: '*And I definitely wasn't in the park on Sunday.*'"

I grabbed Mila by the shoulders. "Of course, that's it! We never *told* her what day Rags was missing! How could she have known it was Sunday?"

Mila glanced at her watch. "There's still time," she said. "If we're right, Rags will be home with you . . . tonight."

On the way back to my house, Mila sang as she rode. That was a good sign. It meant she was happy. And Mila was happiest when we were solving a case. The tune was "London Bridge Is Falling Down." But Mila changed the words around:

"Ragsy is a drooling dog,
drooling dog, drooling dog,
Ragsy is a drooling dog.
Watch out you've been slimed!"

I called Ralphie Jordan right away. He told me the thread didn't match. "Thanks, Ralphie," I told him. "I just needed to be sure. Now I've got one more favor to ask. . . ."

We stashed our bikes behind some bushes and hid. Mila and I watched Ralphie walk up to the yellow house on 41 Lakeview Road. The girl with bangs answered the door. We couldn't hear what Ralphie was saying, but I had a pretty good idea.

See, we needed proof. But Mila and I couldn't be the ones to get it. The girl had already seen us. She knew we were looking for Rags. But Ralphie Jordan was a new face. We told him to knock on the door and say he was on a scavenger hunt. He was supposed to ask for a couple of usual things — a safety pin, a yellow pencil — and one very important item: a piece of thread from a green sweater.

In a few minutes, Ralphie was back, huffing and puffing. He held out the thread, his face beaming with pride.

It was a perfect match.

"She's the one," Mila said, gritting her teeth.

"There's something else," Ralphie added. "When I knocked on the door, I heard barking."

"What kind of barking?" I asked.

Ralphie made a face. "I dunno. Just . . . barking."

"Think, Ralphie," I said. "Was it a yip-yap type of bark? Or more of a woof-woof?"

Ralphie told me it was more of a woof-woof-type bark.

I stood up. "Wait here. I'm going to get Rags."

"Alone?" Mila asked.

"He's my dog," I answered. "My responsibility. I'm going alone."

Chapter Eleven

Family Reunion

All liars are afraid of one thing.

And that's The Truth.

Sure, at first she denied everything. But I had the facts. I had the proof. All the pieces fit together like a jigsaw puzzle. So I planted my feet, crossed my arms, and told her that I wasn't leaving without my dog. "Unless," I said, "you prefer I call the police."

Maybe she was lonely in her new neighborhood. Maybe she always wanted a good dog. Maybe when she saw Rags, she

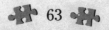

saw a chance to have a big, wonderful pet to love. It didn't matter to me, not really. Because Rags was mine.

She messed with the wrong guy.

"I told my parents he was a stray," she said, half apologizing. "I just wanted to love him. . . ."

"Save the excuses," I interrupted. "And meantime, try the Animal Rescue Shelter. They have dogs that really do need your love."

Getting home was the best part. Rags bounded into the house like a runaway bumper car. He jumped from person to person — leaping at my dad, wrestling with my brothers, licking my sister, Grams, and Mom. Then he jumped on me so hard, he knocked me to the floor. There I was, flat on my back, with Rags sitting on top of me. He licked me in the face over and over.

Being slimed never felt so good.

After things settled down, it was life as

usual in the Jones house. We were a family again. Complete, together. Grams watched her show on television. Billy went "out." Hillary chatted on the phone with friends. Daniel and Nicholas argued over the computer. And I did my homework, with Rags lying by my feet.

It turned out pretty well.

I AM THANKFUL FOR...
1. My family
2. My friends
3. My dog
4. Jigsaw puzzles
5. Mysteries

I found that I couldn't stop at five. I added all kinds of things:

6. Pizza
7. Grape juice

8. Holidays
9. Clues
10. Star Wars
11. Frozen mini-waffles
12. Legos
13. Room 201
14. The New York Mets

For some reason, I began to think about Mr. Signorelli. After all, he helped crack the case. I thought about him in the park, sitting alone at the picnic table.

And I had one last, wonderful idea.

Chapter Twelve

Thanksgiving

It was Thanksgiving morning. My mom and dad were busy making the turkey, with help from Grams and Hillary. My brothers went out to play football in the park.

"Come on, Worm," Nicholas invited. "We could use you."

I told them I had something better to do.

After an hour, I almost gave up. But finally he came, as I knew he would.

"Well, hello there, young fella," Mr. Signorelli said. He sat down at the picnic table opposite me. "I see you found your dog."

"Thanks to you," I said.

"Wasn't nothing," he replied. Then Mr. Signorelli made a clicking sound with his tongue — *tcch, tcch.* In a moment, a few squirrels drew near. But this time they held back, fearful.

"It's your dog," he said, patting Rags on the head. "The squirrels are nervous with him around."

I held the leash tight. "Um, Mr. Signorelli?"

The old man looked at me, waiting.

"What are you doing today? For Thanksgiving, I mean."

He scratched the end of his nose and looked out across the lake. I followed his gaze. But there was nothing there. Just water and emptiness.

He shrugged. "Probably pop a TV dinner in the oven and watch the football games."

"No family?" I asked.

"Kids have grown up, moved away," he explained. "My wife, Sophia, well, she passed on a few years ago."

He looked into the sky, as if searching for a bird that wasn't there.

"You're not smoking today," I noticed.

Mr. Signorelli waved his hand, like swatting away a pesky fly. "Don't make a big deal out of it," he said. "I'm not making any promises. Maybe I'll quit. Maybe I won't. We'll see what happens."

It was now or never. I took a deep breath and talked fast. "We have a great TV. It's perfect for watching football games. And my sister and brothers are nice, most times. I'm sure they'll be nice today, because it's a holiday and they have to. The thing is, I told my parents about you, Mr. Signorelli. They're grateful for your help. . . ."

I was making a mess of it. He didn't understand.

"It's just that . . . well . . . my parents said it's OK and even Grams said it sounded like a terrific idea."

Mr. Signorelli tugged at his coat sleeves. He looked at me questioningly.

Finally I blurted it out. "Would you like to come to our house? For Thanksgiving dinner, I mean. Or maybe just dessert and coffee? My mom makes great pecan pie. You like coffee, don't you, Mr. Signorelli?"

Mr. Signorelli lifted his chin and peered at me over his enormous nose. I watched his eyes flicker, then decide. He reached into his pocket and, with a sweep of his arm, tossed a handful of peanuts to the squirrels. "Happy Thanksgiving, fellas!" he called out to them.

Then he stood up and rubbed his hands across his stomach. "I haven't had pecan pie in years." Mr. Signorelli smiled,

chuckling softly to himself. "You know what? I don't even remember your name."

"Jones," I answered. "Jigsaw Jones."

We walked out of the park together.

Just an old man, a dog on a leash, and me.

"Happy Thanksgiving, Mr. Signorelli," I said.

"Yes, it is," he said. "It really is."

He placed his hand on my shoulder. "Now tell me, Mr. Jones, about this Grams you mentioned. . . ."

My eyes darted up to Mr. Signorelli. He grinned and winked. I had to laugh.

Well, the case was over. I'd solved another mystery — thanks to Mila, my friends, and a kind stranger with hair growing out of his ears.

Go figure.

Maybe Thanksgiving wasn't such a bad holiday after all.

The Case of the
Great Sled Race

For Gavin

Chapter One

Postcard from Florida

I sat at the kitchen table on a Sunday afternoon, warming my hands around a cup of hot chocolate. My toes were wet and cold. My nose was as red as Superman's cape. I was frozen solid, like a human Popsicle. It was the middle of January, and it had been snowing all weekend.

I glanced at the postcard on the table. It showed a white sandy beach, a green ocean, and a neat row of palm trees. Yellow letters floated across a blue sky: LIFE'S A BEACH!

 77

It was a perfect picture of a summer day. Only it wasn't summer. It was Miami. I flipped the card over. It read, *Weather is here. Wish you were wonderful.* That was Aunt Harriet's sense of humor, all right.

Yeesh.

Aunt Harriet was on vacation in Florida. She hated winter. Aunt Harriet complained about the cold, the mittens, the snow, the slush, the whole frozen mess.

Go figure.

Me? I'll take the four seasons anytime: spring, summer, fall, *and* winter. I always have two words for Aunt Harriet:

Snow.

Day.

What could be better? You wake up under thick, warm blankets. Your mom comes into the room and says, "Don't get up. It's a snow day. School's closed."

So the first thing you do is jump out of bed. No classes, no books, no homework.

It's like a mini-vacation. A day for sled rides and snowball fights.

I glanced out the window, saw the fat white flakes drifting from the clouds, and flicked the postcard onto the table. Nope, they didn't have snow days in Florida. I'd have to remind Aunt Harriet next time I saw her.

I gobbled up my grilled cheese sandwich and hustled out the door. I could still get in a lot of sledding if I hurried. I was glad I didn't have any mysteries to solve. I mean, sure, I *loved* being a second-grade detective. And I made good money solving mysteries. But today I was taking the day off. Even a detective needs a break once in a while.

I was dragging my sled into the park when I spotted Bigs Maloney. Bigs was the roughest, toughest kid in second grade — but not taller than a grizzly bear and not

wider than a soda machine. He was headed my way.

Bigs stared straight ahead, mumbling to himself. He stopped in front of me. "Velma," he said. "I want my Velma back. You have to help me find her, Jigsaw."

Bigs put his giant paw on my shoulder.

And squeezed.

"Lay off the shoulder, will you?" I pleaded. "I might need that arm someday."

Bigs let go of my arm. He stared off into the distance. "I just want my Velma back," he said. "You have to help me."

Chapter Two

The Velocity Machine 2000

I led Bigs Maloney into my basement. I sat at my desk. Bigs sat across from me. I watched his gaze dance around the room. His eyes finally rested on the sign behind me.

"Grape juice?" I offered Bigs.

Bigs growled like a big dog. He said he didn't want any lousy grape juice.

I shrugged and poured myself a glass.

"So who's Velma?" I asked.

Bigs gave me a strange look, as if a toucan had just landed on my hat.

"Velma," I repeated, speaking slowly. "Who is she?"

"Velma?" Bigs echoed.

Bigs was pretty shaken up. "Snap out of it, Bigs," I demanded. "What happened out there?"

Bigs glared darkly. I watched his thick fingers curl into fists. "Somebody stole my Velma," Bigs barked. "And you're gonna help me find the crumb who did it."

I ran my fingers through my hair. We'd been together for nearly twenty minutes, and I still didn't know what he was talking about. "Sit here," I told Bigs. "And don't chew on the furniture while I'm gone."

I took the stairs two at a time. Mila answered her phone on the third ring. "I'll be right over," she said.

Five minutes later, Mila was throwing questions at Bigs Maloney. "Who is this Velma you're talking about?" Mila asked. "I thought you liked Lucy Hiller?"

Bigs made a face, like he was disappointed in us. "Velma is a *what*, not a *who*," he said.

"What kind of *what*?" Mila asked.

"A *sled* kind of what — that's who!" Bigs shot back. "My Velocity Machine 2000. The fastest sled in town."

Finally I understood. *Vel*-ocity . . . *Ma*–chine. *Vel-ma*.

"Oh," I said. "Velma is the name of your sled!"

Bigs sneered. "And I'm gonna clobber the crumb who stole her."

Mila gave me a worried look.

Yeesh.

"Listen, Bigs," I said. "I don't think clobbering anybody is such a great idea.

But we'll help you find your sled. You know our rates. We get a dollar a day."

Bigs dug into his front pockets. He pulled out a fistful of soggy dollar bills. He peeled one from the crumpled mess and plastered it on my office desk. George Washington stared up at me.

I picked up the dollar bill and reached out my free hand. "It's a deal." We shook hands.

Mila cleared her throat. "This is all very nice," she said. "But we don't have any clues yet." Mila stared hard into Bigs Maloney's eyes. "Let's hear it, Bigs. Nice and slow. From the beginning. What happened to Velma?"

Chapter Three
The Crime Scene

"Follow me," Bigs answered.

We trudged through the snow. We headed for Lincoln Park, the scene of the crime. It was just a few blocks from my house. When it snowed, Long Hill was the most popular sledding spot in the park. There was a boathouse at the bottom of the hill, where you could rent paddleboats during the summer. In winter, they opened up the building for sledders. People came in to sit around the fire, eat curly french fries, and drink hot chocolate.

"Where'd you see Velma last?" I asked Bigs.

Bigs pointed to a spot beside the boathouse. There were ten or so sleds scattered on a snowbank. "I went inside for a Snickers bar," he said. "I left Velma right here, leaning against the wall. When I came back, she was gone."

"How long were you inside?" Mila asked.

"Ten minutes, maybe fifteen," Bigs said.

"Were you alone?" I asked.

"Yeah, alone," Bigs shot back, his face turning red. "Some bum took my Velma!" Bigs put his hands on his hips and growled. I half expected hot lava to pour from his ears. Bigs stomped around in circles. He packed a fat snowball. Then Bigs whirled and fired. The sun had to duck to get out of the way.

"Nice throw. Feel better now?" I asked.

"Nah," he snarled. "I'll only feel better when I get Velma back." Bigs stepped

forward, towering over me. I stared into his neck. Then I felt a brick crash down on my shoulder. Only it wasn't a brick. It was Bigs Maloney's hand.

"I want that sled back, Jigsaw," Bigs said between clenched teeth. "It's your job to get it back — or else."

Bigs turned and marched toward the hill.

"Or else?" I whispered to Mila. *"Or else what?!* What do you think he means, *or else*?"

Mila just blinked. "I don't know exactly," she said. "But I think it would involve pain."

We caught up with Bigs at the base of the hill. He was watching the sledders race down the slope. His eyes looked moist. I was worried the big lug might burst into tears. Either that, or rip a tree out of the ground.

The hill was crowded with kids. They roared down the hill, screaming happily. A group of parents stood on the ridge. They stamped their feet on the ground, trying to stay warm. Some of them held camcorders. Parents, yeesh. They'll videotape *anything* — baseball games, Halloween parades, birthday parties, the works.

"Look at this," Mila said. She shoved a sheet of paper under my eyes.

Sign up today for...

JIMMY'S SPORTS EMPORIUM'S
2nd ANNUAL SLEDDING CONTEST
January 23. 1:00 P.M.
Singles and Doubles Races.
First Prize: Free Ice-skating Lessons!

"Did you know about this?" I asked Bigs.

"Sure, I knew about it," he answered. "What do you think I was doing here all day — collecting daisies? The races are in one week. And I was gonna win, too. Me and Velma. Nobody could beat us."

Mila and I locked eyes. It was our first clue. We left Bigs a few minutes later. On the way home, I talked over the case with my partner. "Maybe that's why the thief stole Velma," I suggested. "He knew Bigs would win the race."

"He or *she* knew," Mila corrected. "We don't know if the thief is a boy or a girl."

I shrugged. "So he, *or she,* steals the sled. That way Bigs can't be in the race. And the thief has a better chance to win."

"I'll get a list of everyone who signed up for the race," Mila said. "They're all suspects."

Chapter Four
Who, What, Where, When, and Why

The snow stopped falling around dinnertime. My parents seemed relieved. "It looks like you'll be going to school tomorrow," my father happily announced.

My brothers groaned. My sister, Hillary, angrily stabbed at her potatoes. Grams asked me what I'd been learning in school.

"Nothing," I explained.

"Reading any books?" she asked.

"We started one in class last week," I told her. "We're about halfway finished. It's called *Stone Fox* by John . . . Reynolds . . .

Gardiner." I told Grams the story. It was about a boy named Willy. He had a dog, Searchlight. They were just about to enter a dogsled race. Willy had to win or else he'd lose the family farm.

"Sounds good," Grams said.

I told her it wasn't good. "It's *great*."

After dinner, I pulled out my detective journal. I drew a picture of Bigs Maloney. It came out looking like Frankenstein on a bad hair day. In other words, it looked just like Bigs.

I wrote: **THE CASE OF THE GREAT SLED RACE.**

I thought about the type of person who would steal a sled from Bigs Maloney. The thief would have to be brave, big, and tough. And more than a little crazy. Only a nut would mess with Bigs Maloney. It was my job to find the thief. And then, if I could, to stop Bigs from ripping off the poor guy's arms and legs.

I crawled into bed, dead tired. Maybe it would start snowing again. Maybe tomorrow would be a snow day.

Hey, a guy can dream, can't he?

First thing in the morning, I looked out my bedroom window. The sky was sunny and clear. The white snow, reflecting the sun, stung my eyes. There was a knock at the door.

"Up and at 'em, kiddo," my dad gleefully called. "It's not snowing and the roads are open. Better get dressed for school."

Yeesh.

My class is in room 201. Ms. Gleason is the best teacher in the whole school, easy. She's tall and she smiles a lot. In reading circle, we read chapter seven of *Stone Fox*. Ms. Gleason read out loud:

Little Willy needed his rest. So did Searchlight. Tomorrow was going to be a big day. The biggest day of their lives.

Ms. Gleason closed the book. "Tomorrow we'll read chapter eight," she announced.

We all groaned. "Can't you keep reading?" begged Helen Zuckerman.

"Please!" chimed in Joey Pignattano.

"Pretty please," said Ralphie Jordan. "We'll be good all day — even if it kills us!"

Ms. Gleason smiled. "Mr. Gardiner is a terrific writer. But we've got a lot of other work to do." She walked over to the blackboard. Ms. Gleason said, "As you know, we should always be *thinking* while we're reading. That's how we *understand* what's happening in the story. Today I'd like to talk about a few strategies that will help us *think* about what we're reading."

Ms. Gleason told us about *The Five "W" Questions*. Who, what, where, when, and why. She pulled out a big chart and we brainstormed together. The *Who* questions told us about characters. *Where* and *When* told us about the book's setting. *Why* and *What* told about the story, or plot.

I suddenly realized it was like solving a mystery. Reading was like detective work. Figure out the *W* questions . . . and you'll catch the crook.

Chapter Five
Breaking the Code

I found a note in my desk after lunch:

Blue the breezy I'm frog rice rainy getting
fat cat sunny the song freezing list sled
cloudy tonight.

I recognized Mila's handwriting. It was in code. Mila was always testing my brainpower. I studied the note carefully. Then I noticed a pattern. The note used a lot of weather words. *Breezy, rainy, sunny, freezing,* and *cloudy.* We'd just started a weather unit in school. So I knew all about that stuff.

I remembered another code we used. It was a color code. The only words that mattered were the ones that came right after a color word. Maybe this was the same. I circled *breezy, rainy, sunny, freezing,* and *cloudy.* Then I underlined the words that were next.

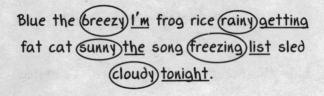

The message read:

I'm getting the list tonight.

Mila was probably going to Jimmy's Sports Emporium. All she had to do was find out who had signed up for the same race as Bigs Maloney. I made eye contact with Mila. I slid my finger across my nose. That was our secret signal. It meant I got the message.

In the afternoon, Ms. Gleason made us answer *W* questions. They were about *Stone Fox*. Ms. Gleason wrote sentences on the blackboard. Then we had to decide if the underlined words told *who, what, when,* or *where.* I wrote down my answers.

Where	1.	Little Willy lived <u>in Wyoming.</u>
When	2.	Grandfather laid in bed for <u>weeks.</u>
What	3.	Searchlight pulled <u>the sled.</u>
Who	4.	<u>Stone Fox</u> never lost a race.

Ms. Gleason gave us ten sentences in all. And you know what? It was just like detective work. I pulled out my journal and scribbled some notes:

WHAT	Velma = Bigs Maloney's sled
WHERE	Long Hill
WHEN	Jan. 16
WHY	Win the race?
WHO	? ? ?

In the detective business, there's another word for "why." It's called *motive*. When you try to guess a criminal's motive, you are really asking *why* they did

something. For instance: Why does someone rob a bank? To get rich. That's the *motive*.

But why steal Bigs Maloney's sled? Mila and I could only guess. We didn't know for sure. Not yet, anyway. Someone probably stole the sled because they wanted to win the race.

One thing was for sure. I wouldn't want to be the thief. Because sooner or later, we'd catch him (or her). We always did. And then he (or she) would have to answer to Bigs Maloney.

Chapter Six

Mila Comes Through

"I've got some bad news, Jigsaw."

It was Mila on the phone.

"You couldn't get the list?" I guessed.

"No, I got the list all right," Mila said. "But we've got our work cut out for us. A lot of kids signed up for that race."

"Do we know any of them?" I asked.

"Sure," Mila answered. "All of 'em. I signed you up, too."

"You what?"

"I signed you up," Mila said. "I had to — that's how I got to see the list. I thought it would seem weird if I just *looked* at the list. So I signed you up. You're in the singles race, ages six to eight. One o'clock on Sunday."

Yeesh. I didn't exactly love the idea of racing against Bigs Maloney. I'd rather go swimming with Orca the Killer Whale.

Mila read the names to me over the phone. I jotted them down in my journal:

Bigs Maloney   Joey Pignattano
Lucy Hiller   Jasper Noonan
Ralphie Jordan   Wingnut O'Brien
Bobby Solofsky   Nicole Rodriguez
Mike Radcliffe   Jigsaw Jones

"Not counting me and Bigs, that makes eight suspects," I said.

I could almost hear Mila nod in agreement.

"Hey, Mila," I said. "Fluff up my memory. Who's Jasper Noonan?"

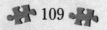

"You know him," Mila scolded. "He's *Stringbean*."

"Oh, Stringbean. I forgot that his real name is Jasper."

"Yep," Mila replied. "Jasper Noonan — also known as Stringbean. The skinniest kid in room 201!"

I thought about Jasper Noonan. I didn't know much about him. Except that he was afraid of bees, thunder, and just about anything that moved.

We agreed to get started first thing tomorrow. We'd have to talk to each suspect. It's what detective work is all about. Talking to witnesses. Looking for clues.

Solving a mystery is like doing a jigsaw puzzle. You start by turning over all the pieces.

I sat across from Nicole during lunch on Tuesday. She already knew about Bigs Maloney's missing sled. "Bigs made a huge scene," Nicole said. Her nose twitched like a rabbit's. She scratched it with her thumb.

"What kind of scene?" I asked.

"You know Bigs," Nicole said, allowing herself a slight smile. "He screamed a lot. Bigs said he'd clobber whoever stole his sled."

"Sounds like Bigs to me," I commented, frowning. "Where were you during all this?"

"Me?" Nicole asked. "I just ignored him.

He's all talk, anyway. I kept right on sledding."

Later on, I managed to talk with Mike Radcliffe and Bobby Solofsky. They said the same thing as Nicole: Bigs Maloney made a big fuss up on the hill. I frowned at the news. That meant the thief was probably scared. Now he'd *really* be hard to find.

When I got back to room 201, I had a surprise waiting for me. But she wasn't wrapped in a bow.

Chapter Seven

Detective Work

Lucy Hiller had curly hair, red boots, a bright purple skirt, and a missing front tooth. She was leaning on my desk when I returned from lunch.

"Can we talk?" she asked.

"We *are* talking," I replied.

"Not here," she said. Lucy pulled on my shirt. "In private. It's about the case."

"Watch the shirt," I complained. "It's a family heirloom."

Lucy looked puzzled.

 114

"A hand-me-down," I explained.

Suddenly, Lucy's eyes widened. I followed her gaze to see a group of kids enter the room. Bigs Maloney was with them. "I'll call you," Lucy whispered. "Tonight."

Lucy hurried back to her seat. I stood there scratching the back of my neck. Why would Lucy Hiller be afraid of Bigs Maloney?

Ms. Gleason read chapter eight of *Stone Fox*. We listened in perfect silence. Everyone was dying to find out what happened next. In the story, the townspeople had gathered to watch the race. But no one thought little Willy could win — except maybe Searchlight, Willy, Doc Smith, and me.

Ms. Gleason read, " '*Mayor Smiley raised a pistol to the sky and fired. The race had begun!*' "

Then she closed the book. "That's all for today."

"What?!" squealed Helen Zuckerman. "You can't stop reading *now*!"

"I'm sorry," Ms. Gleason said. "It's the end of the chapter."

Yeesh. We were all mad at the author. It wasn't fair to end the chapter right in the middle of the action. Ms. Gleason laughed and said it was called a *cliffhanger*. She said, "The author wants to keep you on the edge of your seats. He wants you to hurry up to the next chapter."

Bobby Solofsky said it was a dirty, rotten trick.

"Perhaps," Ms. Gleason replied. "But it works!"

I sat next to Mila on the bus ride home. Mila told me she had talked to two suspects — Ralphie Jordan and Lucy Hiller.

"Anything turn up?" I asked.

"Not exactly," Mila said. "But Lucy seemed . . ."

". . . interested?" I said, finishing her sentence.

Mila's eyes shifted toward me. "Yes, very interested," she said. "Lucy wanted to know *everything* about the case."

"Did you find that odd?" I asked.

"Not really," Mila replied. "I mean, Lucy has always liked Bigs Maloney. I figure she just cares a lot."

I didn't say anything. Maybe that was it.

Maybe Lucy just cared a lot.

Maybe.

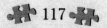 117

But then again, maybe aardvarks played hopscotch on Tuesday nights. I didn't like *maybes*. I wanted facts.

We had doorbells to ring. Wingnut O'Brien was first, because he lived next door to me. We called him Wingnut on account of his ears. They were three sizes too big for his head.

Wingnut said he left Long Hill early on Sunday. "I signed up for the race. Then I went to Freddy Fenderbank's birthday party," he explained.

We shoved on. Nobody was home at Joey Pignattano's. We hit Stringbean's house. Mila knew where he lived. "He's neighbors with Lucy Hiller," she told me.

Jasper Noonan was surprised to see us. I mean, he practically *fainted*. I suppose he wasn't used to having visitors. Jasper didn't even invite us in. Instead, he held the door open a crack and poked his head out. He coughed and sneezed a lot. "I'b all snuffed up," Jasper said. He wiped his nose with his sleeve. Gross me out the door.

Jasper said he was at Long Hill on Sunday. But he didn't see anybody take Velma.

"Were you alone?" Mila asked.

Jasper's eyes flickered. "Yeth," he answered. "Why? Do you tink I stole it?"

I waved the thought away. "No, Jasper. We're just asking a few questions. Thanks for your help." Mila and I turned to leave.

"Is Bigs still . . . mad?" Jasper asked.

We stopped in our tracks.

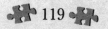

"Bigs seebed really mad . . . up on the hill," Jasper said through his stuffed-up nose. "He said id was clobbering tibe."

Clobbering time. I forced a smile. "That's Bigs Maloney for you."

"Do you thik he would really . . . clobber . . . sobebody?" Jasper asked.

A sudden wind crept up. Jasper shivered.

"Yes," I answered. "Bigs would."

Jasper's face turned white. His eyes grew watery. Then he sneezed hard enough to knock the glasses off his nose.

Poor guy.

He sure caught a bad cold.

At least I *think* it was a cold.

Anyway, it was a bad case of something.

Chapter Eight

A Call from Lucy

After our visit with Stringbean, it was time to get home. So we did. It gets dark early in January. Mila and I didn't have much to say about the case. We both knew we needed another clue. We talked about *Stone Fox* instead. Mila said it was a great work of *literature*. That's Mila for you. Sometimes she likes to use grown-up words. I don't hold it against her. I told Mila that *Stone Fox* was the best work of literature I'd read since *Captain Underpants and the Attack of the Talking Toilets.*

Mila rolled her eyes.

Go figure.

I was working on my homework when the phone rang. It was Lucy Hiller.

"Hi, Lucy." I wondered what she wanted. "What do you want?" I asked.

"Um, like, nothing," she said.

"Oh," I answered. "Well, bye. I guess I'll talk to you later."

"Wait!" she said.

I waited. Finally I said, "Look, Lucy. You called because you wanted to tell me something. So go ahead. Tell me something."

Lucy took a deep breath. "Um, like, I was wondering how the case was going. Any suspects?"

"A few," I lied.

"Anyone I know?" she asked.

The question floated by like a bubble. I didn't pop it. Lucy asked a few more questions about the sled. I answered most

of them with a shrug. On the phone, that's not real helpful. But then again, I wasn't trying to be helpful. I had a picture of George Washington in my pocket that said I was working for Bigs Maloney. Not Lucy Hiller.

"Why do *you* care so much?" I asked her.

"No reason," Lucy said. "Just curious."

I sure was. I hung up the phone and wrote in my journal:

WHY IS LUCY SO CURIOUS?
DID SHE STEAL THE SLED?

Next morning, I caught up with Joey Pignattano at the bus stop. In the detective business, you learn a lot about people. Sometimes one small fact will tell you a lot about a guy. For example: Joey Pignattano once ate a live, wriggling worm for a dollar. That's about all you need to know about Joey Pignattano. He was a worm-eating kind of guy. But I liked him anyway. He always seemed like an honest person.

Still, there was the problem of a missing sled named Velma.

I had to keep asking questions. Sooner or later somebody would come up with an answer I liked.

"I didn't do it!" Joey told me. "And I can prove it!"

"Prove it?" I asked. "How?"

 125

"My parents were there the whole time. They can vouch for me," Joey said.

I stamped my feet to keep out the cold. I remembered all the parents on top of Long Hill. I remembered . . . camcorders. "By any chance, were your parents making a video?"

Joey beamed. "How did you guess that?"

"Dumb luck," I said. "Can I watch it?"

Joey shrugged. "I guess so. Why?"

"Why?" I repeated. "*Why?!* I'm not sure, Joey. I'm still working on who, what, when, and where."

Chapter Nine
The Video Clue!

I couldn't wait for the school day to end. I wanted to get to Joey's house and watch that video. I had a feeling that it might hold a clue that could break the case wide open. Meanwhile, I was trapped in school. But the day wasn't all bad. Ms. Gleason read the last two chapters of *Stone Fox*. The ending was happy *and* sad. I noticed that even Bigs Maloney cried a little.

That was a mistake.

Because Bigs *noticed* that *I* noticed. A few minutes later, he came over to my desk.

Bigs jabbed a finger into my chest. *Ping*. It felt like an aluminum baseball bat. "I paid you," he said. "Now I want my Velma back."

"Easy on the chest, will you, Bigs? I store my heart in there."

Bigs frowned.

Ping. He jabbed me again.

Mila stepped between us. "We've just about solved the case, Bigs! You'll have Velma back by tomorrow!" she promised.

"Really?" Bigs asked.

Mila gave Bigs her biggest smile. "Really," she said. I noticed that her fingers were crossed behind her back.

An enormous grin filled Bigs Maloney's face. He was suddenly as happy as a puppy with a new chew toy. *Whack!* His giant hand slapped my back. My eyeballs nearly rolled across the floor. "Thanks a lot, you guys!" Bigs shouted. "Thanks a million! Thanks a . . . thanks . . . a . . . *gazillion*!" Then he walked away. I mean, *maybe* he walked. I don't know for sure. The big lug was so happy he might have floated away on fluffy white clouds.

I looked at Mila. She shrugged back at me. "I had to tell him something," she explained.

"I guess," I said.

"Bigs is a little rough," Mila observed.

"Yeah, I noticed," I said, rubbing my chest. "But it's not easy losing something

you love. Even if it's only a sled. Remember when I lost Rags?"

Mila remembered. How could she forget? *I was a total mess. My dog was lost for three whole days.*

"I think that's how Bigs feels right now," I said. "The big hockey puck doesn't know what to do. I feel sorry for the guy. Bigs talks tough. But have you ever *seen* him actually hurt anybody?"

Mila thought it over. "Come to think of it, no."

"See," I said. "Bigs doesn't really *want* to clobber anybody. It's like he says. He just wants his Velma back."

We rushed over to Joey's house after school. Mila even brought a bag of popcorn for everyone to share. Oh, brother. It wasn't like we were watching Nickelodeon. This was a home movie of Joey Pignattano rolling around in the snow.

And making goofy faces.

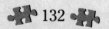

And sledding down the hill.

And walking up the hill.

And picking his nose.

And sledding down the hill. Then up again. Then down. Up. Down. Up.

After half an hour, I asked Joey, "Exactly how long *is* this video?"

He told me it was almost over.

I hoped he was right.

The movie played on. Meanwhile, I tried to decide which was worse: watching

Joey's home movie . . . or having a tooth pulled.

With rusty pliers.

I was still trying to decide when something caught my eye. "Stop the tape," I demanded.

Joey stopped the tape.

"Rewind."

Joey rewound the tape.

"There!" I said. "Stop right there."

Joey pressed the pause button. I stared at the picture for a solid minute.

I clicked off the television. "We've got 'em."

Chapter Ten

In Jasper's Room

I placed a phone call to Lucy Hiller. I told her we were on our way to Jasper Noonan's house. I told Lucy that I knew Jasper stole the sled. I also told her that Bigs was going to clobber him.

I wasn't exactly telling the truth.

I waited about half an hour before doing push-ups on Jasper's doorbell.

Jasper answered the door. He looked at me and Mila. Jasper peered behind us — and to the sides. It was like he was looking for Bigs Maloney.

And he was.

I was sure that Lucy had already gotten to him.

"It's just us," I said. "Let's talk."

Jasper swallowed hard. He led me and Mila into his bedroom. It looked more like a planetarium. The room was painted black. It had stars and planets painted on the ceiling and walls. It was weird . . . and strange . . . and totally cool.

"Wow," I said.

"Spacey," Mila observed.

Jasper just stood by, fidgeting nervously.

"I think you know why we're here, Stringbean." I told him it was time for the truth.

Jasper sat down on the bed. He held his head in his hands. He finally stared up at me. He was trying to decide something.

Could he trust me . . . or not?

"Let's just *suppose* somebody took the

sled," Jasper finally said. He didn't quite look me in the eye.

"Sure, Jasper," I said. "We could play it that way. Let's suppose."

"And let's *suppose*," he continued, "that this *person* only meant to borrow it."

I nodded. "Keep talking, Jasper."

"Bigs was mad when he couldn't find his sled," Jasper said. "*Real* mad. I'd bet the

person who borrowed the sled might be afraid to return it."

I didn't bite. But I saw the worm on the hook. "So?" I said.

"So," Jasper echoed. "Just suppose somebody still *had* the sled. Even if he *wanted* to return it, maybe he'd be afraid to — because Bigs would pound him into dust."

I took the bait. "You wouldn't happen to *be* this person, would you, Jasper?"

Jasper looked down. He bit his lip. He untucked his shirt and tucked it back in again. "No, I mean, of course not. I was just supposing."

Oh, brother.

"Well, let's suppose this," I said. "Let's suppose I get Bigs Maloney over here. Let's suppose I tell Bigs that you stole Velma. What do you *suppose* Bigs Maloney might do?"

Jasper turned pale. He started to stammer.

"That's enough, Jigsaw!"

The voice came from behind the closet door.

Lucy Hiller stepped out.

"Don't look so surprised," she told me. "I've been hiding here all the time."

"I'm *not* surprised," I answered. "In fact, I was counting on it."

It was Lucy's turn to look surprised.

I continued, "That's why I called you first, Lucy. I knew you were in on it with Jasper." I held up the videotape. "Joey's parents like to make home movies," I explained. "Boring stuff, most of it. Except for one little scene. A scene that stars Jasper — and you, Lucy. Remember? It was last Sunday afternoon. Near Long Hill. When you two went off with Bigs Maloney's Velocity Machine 2000."

Lucy started to argue. "But . . ."

I held up my hand. "It's all on tape. There's no use denying the facts. I know *who,* and *what,* and *when,* and *where.* But I don't know *why.*"

I paused. "So finish the puzzle for me," I said. *"Why did you take Bigs Maloney's sled?"*

Chapter Eleven
The Great Sled Race

"I knew you'd make trouble, Jigsaw," Lucy muttered. "The minute Bigs hired you, I knew you'd make trouble."

"I'm a detective," I replied. "Trouble is my business."

Lucy put a hand on Jasper's shoulder. "I'm sorry, Stringbean," she said. "I can't protect you anymore."

Jasper looked like a sick puppy. If he had a tail, it would have been between his legs.

"I don't get it," Mila said. "Why did you steal the sled, Lucy?"

Lucy shook her head. "Nobody *stole* the sled," she answered. "Stringbean only borrowed it without asking, sort of."

Jasper sniffed and looked up at Lucy. He spoke up. "I just wanted to try it. Just once. It looked so cool."

A lightbulb went off over my head. I saw it all clearly. "But Bigs noticed the sled was gone before you could return it," I said. "He started making threats . . ."

". . . and I got scared," Jasper confessed. "I hid the sled in the bushes."

It was Lucy's turn to talk. "I saw what happened," she admitted. "I've been neighbors with Stringbean all my life. He's not a thief. I didn't want Bigs to hurt him. So I helped Jasper hide the sled."

She looked at Mila, then at me. Right in the eye. "That's the truth."

I believed her.

"You still have the sled?" I asked.

Jasper nodded.

"I'll take it off your hands," I said. "But I won't tell Bigs where I got it. You don't have anything to be afraid of."

"But what if Bigs finds out?" Jasper asked.

"Don't worry," I answered. "I'll handle Bigs Maloney. He just wants his sled back."

* * * * *

It was the day of the big race. So we all piled on the layers — long underwear and itchy sweaters — and climbed Long Hill.

Mila towed a sled, too. Of course, Mila hadn't mentioned that she signed us up for the doubles race, too. "Let's win," she said. "Why not?"

I smiled at her through my scarf. "Why not!"

The Velocity Machine 2000 lived up to expectations. Bigs easily won the singles race. Ralphie Jordan came in second. Bigs

never suspected a thing. He had his Velma back — it was all that mattered. He really wasn't the clobbering type.

Who won the doubles race?

Well, with a partner like Mila . . . how could a guy lose?

Afterward we all went inside for curly fries and hot chocolates. Joey Pignattano's parents made a video of the whole thing. I was happy with the way things turned out.

Bigs got his sled back.

Mila and I won free skating lessons.

And nobody got hurt.

Hey, what did you expect? They don't call me the best detective in second grade for nothing!

The Case of the
Stinky Science Project

Chapter One

Sally-Ann Simms

The pink bows didn't fool me. I ignored the matching lace socks and the little red plastic pocketbook. I knew that Sally-Ann Simms was one tough cookie.

So what if she was only four and a half years old.

Sally-Ann stood in my backyard, hands on her hips. She shouted up to my tree house, "Jigsaw Jones! You up there?"

I was up there — and I told her so. "Take the ladder," I called down. "The elevator's broken."

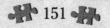 151

Sally-Ann scooted up the ladder. "Your sister, Hillary, said I could find you here," Sally-Ann said.

I held out a paper cup. "Grape juice?" I offered.

Sally-Ann sat down, cross-legged. She grabbed the cup and drained it, slurping loudly. A purple mustache formed over her upper lip. Eyes wide, she looked around. "It's nice up here. It feels like I'm in a bird's nest."

"My dad built it," I explained. "It's kind of wobbly. But he promises it won't fall down." I rapped on a wall with my knuckles. "I hope he's right."

Sally-Ann fished in her little red pocketbook. She pulled out a windup Tarzan toy. She carefully placed it in front of me. "I talked to Wingnut O'Brien," Sally-Ann began. "He said you could help me."

I smiled. "Yeah, good old Wingnut. I found his lost hamster a while back. For a dollar a day, I make problems go away." I frowned at Sally-Ann's empty cup. "More grape juice?"

She nodded. "I don't have much money," Sally-Ann said.

"How much is *not much*, exactly?" I asked.

Sally-Ann fidgeted with her lace socks. "Zero dollars and zero cents."

You didn't need a calculator to do the math. I picked up the Tarzan toy. It was the

kind you get for free with a Happy Meal. One of his arms was missing. "And you hope to pay me . . . *with this*?" I asked. I handed Tarzan back to her. "Sorry, but I've got enough broken toys."

Sally-Ann stared into my eyes. She sighed and got up to leave. That's when I knew I was going to take the case. For free. I just couldn't say no to eyes like that.

Here's the thing. Sally-Ann Simms might have been four feet tall — if she stood on a box and jumped. And the little squirt needed help. *My* help.

Jigsaw Jones, Private Eye.

I reached for Tarzan again. "I guess he's okay," I said. "Let me get my partner. Then you can tell us both all about your problem."

"Thanks, Jigsaw," Sally-Ann said. "I'm sorry I don't have any money. It's just . . ."

"Just . . . what?" I asked.

"It's just that . . . I had to give my ice-cream money to Bobby Solofsky," Sally-Ann said.

I chewed on that for a minute. It left a bad taste in my mouth. Yeah, I thought. Solofsky's just the type to take Popsicle money from a four-year-old.

Chapter Two

Tricked!

Mila Yeh was my best friend and partner. Always had been. She worked with me on all the tough cases. The easy ones, too. She hurried over when I called.

We could hear Mila singing from around the house. Mila was *always* singing something. But she usually changed the words. Today, she was singing "Yellow Submarine" by the Beatles, sort of:

"We all live in a purple submarine,
purple submarine, purple submarine."

 157

Mila bent over, picked up a rock, and hurled it at a tree. *Bull's-eye!* She began singing again:

> *"We all swim in a washing machine,*
> *washing machine, washing machine."*

"Hi, guys," Mila said, greeting us. She sprawled on the tree house floor and poured herself a cup of grape juice.

"Help yourself," I offered.

"Thanks," Mila replied, beaming. "I just did." She looked at me. "So what's up?"

"We were waiting for you," I said. "Something about Bobby Solofsky."

Mila turned to Sally-Ann. "Solofsky, huh? We've had trouble with him before. Can you tell me what happened?"

"Bobby tricked me and took my ice-cream money," Sally-Ann declared. "I want it back!"

Mila gently placed her hand on Sally-Ann's shoulder. "What do you mean, he tricked you?" she asked.

Sally-Ann seemed upset. I offered her a box of Kleenex. I thought it was a nice thing to do. Sally-Ann didn't see it that way.

"I'm not a crybaby," Sally-Ann scoffed.

"Sure," I said. "I just thought . . ."

Sally-Ann glared at me. "Don't treat me like a baby," she said. "Just get my money back!"

 159

She was something, that Sally-Ann Simms. A walking hurricane in lavender and pink.

I opened my detective journal to a clean page. Using bright pink marker in honor of Sally-Ann's lace socks, I wrote: **Client: Sally-Ann Simms.**

"I'm all ears," I said.

Sally began, "I was having a tea party with Mr. Bear and Lady Snuggles and . . ."

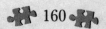

"*Lady Snuggles?*" I asked.

Sally-Ann fixed me with a stare. "Yeah, Lady Snuggles. My stuffed doll. You got a problem with that?"

I stammered, "No, er, I just . . ."

"You just . . . *what?*" Sally-Ann asked sharply.

"Never mind," I said. "What happened next?"

"Bobby came by," she said, turning to

Mila. "He was bragging that he had magical powers."

Mila raised an eyebrow. "Magical powers? Bobby Solofsky?"

Sally-Ann nodded. "I didn't believe him, either. Then he took out a book and a balloon."

I held up my hand. "What color balloon?"

"Red, I think," Sally-Ann said. "Who cares?"

"I do," I said. "It may be a clue. Was the balloon blown up?"

"No, it was . . . *un-blown up*," Sally-Ann remembered. "He said he could move the book with just a balloon."

"Don't tell me you bet him," I said.

Sally-Ann cast her eyes downward. I had my answer. "It's the oldest trick in town," I explained. "He used air pressure to lift the book."

Sally-Ann shook her head. "I don't know

about that. He just put the balloon under the book and blew it up."

Mila spoke up. "The book moved and you had to pay up."

Sally-Ann nodded unhappily.

After Sally-Ann left, Mila and I talked about the case. "It doesn't look good," I said. "It was a fair bet."

"I *suppose*," Mila said. "But it's still a rotten trick. Sally-Ann's not even in kindergarten."

I scribbled a quick picture in my journal. It showed a blown-up balloon underneath a book. Too bad it turned out looking like a fish wearing a bad hat. "I'll have a talk with

Bobby in school tomorrow," I told her. "But I don't think it will do much good."

"You'll figure out something," Mila said. "You always do." She climbed down the ladder and skipped away, singing:

"We all live in a yellow marshmallow, yellow marshmallow, yellow marshmallow!"

Chapter Three
Mila's Secret Code

I sat next to Mila on the school bus Monday morning.

She leaned close to my ear. "I made up a new code last night." Mila liked to test my brainpower with secret codes.

"Great," I said. "Hand it over."

"This one is a brain buster!" Mila warned. "It might make your head *explode*."

"Try me," I offered.

She handed me a piece of paper torn from a notepad.

4 marshmallows
6 coffee cups
3 coconuts
6 peppers
4 blueberries
4 tarts
1 cookie
3 spoons
3 TV dinners
2 lemons

"I think you made a mistake, Mila," I said. "This looks like a shopping list."

Mila smiled. "I know it *looks* like a shopping list. You've got to look harder," she said.

I stared at the list for a long time. I had to admit it. I was bamboozled.

 166

"Do you need a hint?" Mila asked.

I frowned. "I'll figure it out," I said. I didn't want Mila to get the best of me. I studied the code some more. It sure made a strange shopping list. I mean, who buys only four marshmallows? And why would someone want just three spoons? It didn't make any sense.

I shoved the note in my pocket.

"Give up?" Mila asked.

"No, I don't give up," I replied. "But this one might take a little time. My brain needs a rest. Besides," I told her, "you don't really want my head to explode, do you?"

Mila shook her head. "Nah. Too messy."

I opened my detective journal. I drew a self-portrait. It showed my head exploding into pieces. It was a pretty good picture, even though the lines were wobbly. Drawing on a bus isn't the easiest thing in the world.

I showed Mila the picture. It made her laugh. "Definitely too messy," she said.

We heard loud laughter from the back of the bus. It was Bobby Solofsky. He was

horsing around with Eddie Becker and Mike Radcliffe.

"Do you want me to talk to Bobby?" Mila asked.

I shook my head. "I'll do it," I said. "Later on. I've already got one headache this morning. I don't need another."

The bus dropped us off at school. I stuffed the journal in my backpack. Meantime, I kept wondering about that code. Four marshmallows? Two lemons?

Four blueberries? What could someone cook with four blueberries? Maybe that was the trick. Maybe the list was a recipe for something.

Oh, brother.

I knew that my head couldn't explode. Not really. But just in case, I pulled my baseball cap down tight. Yeesh. This time, Mila was *really* testing my brainpower!

Chapter Four

The Volcano

There was a big crowd gathered by the front doors. Helen Zuckerman, Geetha Nair, and Danika Starling were carrying . . . *a mountain*!

"Outta the way!" hollered Helen. "Coming through!"

Mila and Ralphie Jordan held open the doors.

"What's that?" asked Athena Lorenzo.

"Our science project," Helen said.

Ralphie looked worried. "Science project?! Did you say *science project*?!

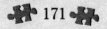

Uh-oh — I knew I should pay more attention in class. Nobody told *me* about any science projects!"

Geetha laughed. "Don't worry, Ralphie. This is our independent project. We did it for extra credit."

Ralphie wiped his hand across his forehead. "Whew!" he exclaimed. The smile returned to his face. "But why did you build a mountain?"

"It's a volcano," Helen corrected him.

That got us all buzzing. A volcano — awesome. Everybody loved volcanoes. Besides, we'd been talking about them in class.

"Will it spew hot lava?" Bigs Maloney asked hopefully.

Danika smiled. "Just wait and see," she said in a singsongy voice. "We're going to show it to everybody in class."

Bigs took that as a definite yes. He

pumped his fist in the air. "All right! Hot molten lava! I can't wait!"

Our teacher, Ms. Gleason, stood in the doorway to room 201. She waved her arms. "This way, girls. Careful now. Watch out for my — *ouch!* — foot."

"Whoops! Sorry about that, Ms. Gleason," Helen apologized.

They placed the volcano on a table in the hallway. "This way, everyone can admire

it," Ms. Gleason said. We all gathered around to take a closer look.

"Please take your seats, children," Ms. Gleason said. "Tomorrow the girls will give us a little demonstration — because their volcano *really works*!"

Everyone cheered. We couldn't wait.

Unfortunately, we had to wait. But we did get to talk more about volcanoes.

"Can anyone name the three different kinds of volcanoes?" Ms. Gleason asked.

Danika Starling's hand shot up.

Ms. Gleason looked around the room. "Anyone else? We talked about this on Friday."

Danika waved her hand desperately. Ms. Gleason finally nodded in her direction.

"Active, dormant, and . . . um, extinct," Danika answered.

"Nice job, Danika," Ms. Gleason said. She wrote the words on the blackboard:

ACTIVE
DORMANT
EXTINCT

Ms. Gleason pointed to the word ACTIVE. "An active volcano may erupt at any time. There are about five hundred active volcanoes in the world," she said.

"Cool!" yelled Mike Radcliffe.

"Not exactly, Mike," Ms. Gleason replied with a smile. "Volcanoes are hot — very, very hot. The molten rock inside a volcano, called *lava*, can be two thousand degrees!"

We all thought that was pretty cool. I mean, *hot*.

"*Dormant* is another word for sleeping," Ms. Gleason told us. "A dormant volcano is sleeping. It has not erupted in a long time. Sometimes for thousands of years. But scientists think it still might one day."

She pointed to the word EXTINCT. "Can

anyone guess what an extinct volcano is like?"

Ralphie Jordan grabbed his throat and made choking noises. "It's dead!" he said. "Like the dinosaurs!"

"Wonderful, Ralphie," Ms. Gleason said. "An extinct volcano will probably never erupt again."

"Bummer!" Eddie Becker complained.

"Let's hope *our* dormant volcano will wake up tomorrow!" Ms. Gleason said. "Right, girls?"

She winked at Helen, Geetha, and Danika.

"Hot, burning lava," Bigs shouted. "Yippee!"

Chapter Five

Bobby and Yoda

In the cafeteria, I heard Bigs Maloney ask Bobby Solofsky a question. Bigs wondered, "Have you gone bonkers?"

Bobby didn't answer.

So Bigs jerked a thumb the size of a pickle toward me. "Tell him," he ordered Bobby.

Bobby made a face. "I said Spider-Man could beat Yoda in a fight."

"Yoda?" I asked. "Big ears, Jedi Master, talks like Grover from *Sesame Street*?"

Bobby nodded.

 179

"No way!" Bigs roared. "Yoda has the Force!"

"Yoda," Bobby replied, "has more wrinkles than a dried prune."

Outraged, Bigs pounded a fist on the table. The table, amazingly, didn't break in half. "Yoda would win, easy!" he said.

Bobby took a big bite of his tuna fish sandwich. I could tell it was tuna fish — because I had a good view of it. Bobby chewed with his mouth open. It wasn't a pretty sight.

"Have you ever seen him walk?" Bobby asked. "The guy's, like, nine million years old. Yoda can barely move. How could he fight?"

"Yoda is a Jedi Master!" Bigs argued. "He trained Luke Skywalker and Qui-Gon Jinn!"

Bobby just shook his head. "Have you *looked* at Yoda's arms? Have you? He couldn't lift my lunch box!"

I could see Bigs Maloney's face turn red. I

tried changing the subject. "Uh, guys," I said. "This is very interesting. But I'm on a case."

Bobby yawned. "Big deal."

I pulled out my journal. "I need to ask you a few questions, Bobby."

Bobby smirked. "Ask away," he said. "I didn't do nothing to nobody."

I looked at Bigs. "Sorry, Bigs. This is private."

Bigs shrugged and walked away. That left me alone with Bobby Solofsky. Oh, joy. "I had a visit from Sally-Ann Simms," I began. "She says you tricked her."

Bobby opened his mouth in fake surprise. "Me? Trick Sally-Ann? I won that money fair and square, *Theodore*."

He called me Theodore just to bug me. It worked. I was bugged.

Bobby continued, "I said I could make a book move by using only a balloon. I won the bet. Fair and square."

I reminded him that Sally-Ann was only four years old.

"So?" Bobby said. He had all the sympathy of a tarantula.

I sighed. "Okay, Solofsky. I guess you win. But next time, try tricking someone your own age."

Bobby folded his hands behind his head. "Sure thing, *Theodore*. Tell you what. I've been working on an amazing new magic trick. Why don't *you* bet me. If you win, I'll give Sally-Ann's money back."

"And if I lose?" I asked.

Bobby flashed a toothy smile. "I get to use your tree house — *for a whole week*."

Chapter Six
The Mysterious Floating Egg

I may have blinked. I'm not sure. The thought of Bobby Solofsky using my tree house gave me the creeps. "What's the trick?" I asked.

Bobby smiled, like a fisherman who feels a tug on the line. Now he wanted to reel me in. He said, "I can float an egg in a jar of water."

"What do you mean?" I asked. "*On* the water?"

"No, *in* the water," Bobby said. "Let me borrow a piece of paper."

Bobby drew a picture of a glass jar filled with water. Right in the middle, he drew an egg. "It won't sink," he said.

"Plain drinking water?" I asked.

Bobby nodded. "Is it a bet?" His eyes twinkled with delight.

Luckily, the school bell rang. It was time to get back to class. "I'll let you know tomorrow," I told him.

Bobby tried to hide his disappointment. "Sure, *Theodore*," he said. "But I hope you bet me. I've always liked that tree house of yours."

I guess Ms. Gleason was still on her science kick. That afternoon she reminded us about the scientific method. "Remember what I told you before, when we did our experiments with mealworms," she said. "A scientist is like a detective."

My ears perked up.

She continued, "The world is full of mystery. Scientists try to discover the truth. They ask questions. They investigate. They try to learn facts. Scientists do this by using the scientific method."

Ms. Gleason handed out sheets of paper. They read:

THE SCIENTIFIC METHOD

1. Identify the problem. <u>What do you want to know?</u>
2. Gather information. <u>What do you already know?</u>
3. Make a prediction. <u>What do you think will happen?</u>
4. Test the prediction. <u>Experiment!</u>
5. Draw a conclusion based on what you learned. <u>Why did the experiment work out the way it did?</u>

I decided that she was right. A scientist *was* like a detective. Only without secret disguises and invisible ink.

After school, I visited Sally-Ann Simms. I had to tell her about my talk with Bobby Solofsky. But first, Sally-Ann introduced me to her stuffed animals.

"Say hello to Mr. Bear and Lady Snuggles," she said.

I mumbled something.

Sally-Ann made a sour face. "Louder," she demanded. "Lady Snuggles can't hear you."

Maybe I said hello to Lady Snuggles. I don't exactly remember. Then I told Sally-Ann the bad news. Bobby wasn't giving the money back.

"I don't care about the money," she shot back. "You can keep the money. I just don't want Bobby to have it. He doesn't play fair."

I tried to explain that life wasn't a bowl of cherries. "I hate cherries," Sally-Ann replied. "Besides, you help *everybody*. Now help me. *Please*."

Yeesh.

I dragged myself over to Mila's.

"Jigsaw!" Mila greeted me. "Did you solve the code?"

"Actually, I could use your help on something else," I said. I told her about Bobby's floating egg trick. She listened closely. "Do you think I should make the bet?"

Mila pulled on her long black hair. "Let's try it ourselves," she suggested.

We went back to my house. I found a glass jar in the kitchen closet. We filled the jar with water. I dropped an egg into the water.

Plop!

It sank like a stone.

Chapter Seven

Thinking Like a Scientist

I tried another egg.

Plop.

It sank, too.

"I have a prediction," I announced. *"Eggs don't float."*

"Maybe we should experiment some more," Mila said. "Just to test your *prediction*."

I pulled out the whole carton of eggs. Two of them dropped on the floor. *Cra-ack.*

"Gross!" Mila said. "You stepped in it."

"Shhh!" I held a finger to my lips. "My mom's in the next room."

I cleaned up the mess. Most of it, anyway. The floor was still a little sticky. And so were my socks. Mila and I returned to the experiment. Every egg fell to the bottom of the jar.

"I was wondering," Mila said, rocking back and forth in her chair. "Was the egg supposed to be regular or *hard-boiled*?"

"We didn't discuss eggs," I said.

So we decided to experiment with hard-boiled eggs. After all, it's what a scientist would do. Only this time, we needed help from a grown-up.

I found my mom in the living room. She was reading a thick book. My big, lazy dog, Rags, was asleep by her feet. "Better than slippers," my dad always said.

"Hey, Mom. Could you make me a hard-boiled egg?"

She waved her hand like a magic wand. "Presto! You're a hard-boiled egg."

"Very funny, Mom," I groaned. "But could you?"

She looked up in surprise. Even Rags looked up. He seemed surprised, too. "I didn't know you *liked* hard-boiled eggs," Mom said.

"It's not to eat," I said. "We're doing an experiment."

"Uh-oh," she said. "Are you two making a mess in there?"

"No, honest," I said. "We're just trying to think like scientists."

"And how does a scientist think?" she asked.

I sighed. Parents, yeesh. Kids have to explain *the simplest things* to them.

"It's like this," I explained. "You have to use something called the scientific method. First you make a *hypothesis*. That's a big word. It means guess, I think. Then you test it, by *experimenting*. Then you draw a *conclusion* based on the facts."

"I see," she said. "But what does this have to do with a hard-boiled egg?"

"Please, Mom," I begged. "It's important."

My mother stood up and stretched. "Okay, kiddo. One hard-boiled egg, coming up."

"Thanks, Mom."

She bent down and gave me a quick kiss. "Sure thing, Mr. Thomas Edison. Since you asked so nicely."

She even boiled *a few* eggs for us, just in case. Each one sank to the bottom. "I'm ready to draw my conclusion," I told Mila. "*Eggs definitely don't float in water.* There's no way Bobby can make an egg float."

"I *suppose* not," Mila said. "But what if Bobby pulls a fast one?"

"What can he do?" I asked. "It's just a jar, some water, and an egg. You don't really think he has magical powers, do you?"

Mila didn't answer. She just rocked back and forth. Softly, she said to herself, "Something's wrong. There's a trick to this. But I don't know what." She stood up to leave. "Gotta go, Jigsaw. Talk to you later."

"Where are you going?" I asked.

Mila smiled. "To speak with an expert."

Chapter Eight
Cracking the Code

Mila called me later that night. "It's a trick," she said. "Bobby probably puts salt in the water. Salt makes the water more dense, so things float easier."

"How do you know?" I asked.

"I talked to my father. He reminded me about our trip to Cape Cod last summer," she said.

"What does that have to do with anything?" I asked.

"We swam a lot," Mila said. "It's easy to float in the ocean. Salt water, you know."

Now I understood. "But Bobby said *plain drinking water*."

"Can't be," Mila insisted. "We did the experiments. We *proved* that eggs don't float in plain water."

We agreed to keep a close eye on Bobby Solofsky. If he tried something sneaky, we'd catch him. After doing my homework, I relaxed by working on a puzzle. It was called "Mummies of Egypt." My oldest brother, Billy, walked into the living room. He was humming.

"I'm going out," he announced.

"Out *where*?" my mom asked.

Billy shrugged. "Just . . . *out*."

My mom frowned. She squinched her nose and sniffed. "What's that smell?"

"Nothing," Billy quickly answered. "I don't smell anything. Do you smell anything, Jigsaw?"

I shook my head. I didn't smell anything. I didn't even *want* to smell anything. I

mean, who wants to smell a teenager?

My mom sniffed Billy's shirt. "Is that . . . your father's aftershave lotion?"

"Aw, Mom," Billy complained.

"And your hair," she said, stepping back. "It's . . . it's . . . *combed*."

Billy's face turned red. "Is not," he protested.

"Who are you going out with?" she asked.

"Karla."

My mom raised an eyebrow. "A girl?"

Billy messed his hair with his hands. He fled toward the door.

"Have a nice" — the door slammed shut — "*time*," my mom called out.

She looked at me and shook her head.

I shook mine right back.

"Teenagers," I muttered.

My dad read to me at bedtime. After he left, I turned on my flashlight. I unfolded the secret code Mila had given me. Rags lay curled beside me as I stared at it.

4 marshmallows
6 coffee cups
3 coconuts
6 peppers
4 blueberries
4 tarts
1 cookie
3 spoons
3 TV dinners
2 lemons

I was starting to wish that I let Mila give me a hint after all. I closed my eyes and tried to think.

Then it hit me. The numbers! It must be something to do with the numbers. Maybe

they held the secret to the code. I opened
my journal and copied the list over. Then I
grabbed a yellow marker.

4 marshmallows

Hmmm.

I counted to the fourth letter. I circled
the "s" in marshmallows. Maybe that was
it. Maybe the number was a clue. I looked
at the next item on the list: 6 coffee cups. I
counted six letters and circled the "e" in
coffee.

I was finally getting somewhere. This was
one of Mila's coolest codes yet. In the end,
it read: *Secret Code*.

Not anymore!

Chapter Nine
I Hate Egg Salad

It was Tuesday. I was in the cafeteria, sitting across from Joey Pignattano.

"I hate egg salad," Joey complained.

My jaw nearly hit the table. "But Joey, you'll eat *anything*! You ate a worm once."

"I draw the line at egg salad," Joey said. He held out the sandwich. "You want it?"

"I don't even want to *look* at it," I said, holding my nose. "Take it away. It stinks."

Joey placed the sandwich on the table. I watched his eyes slide over to the garbage cans. Then back to the egg salad. Then

across the room to the lunch monitor —
who was staring right at him.

Joey had a problem all right. Because
today was Tuesday. His mother was lunch
monitor on Tuesdays.

"Uh-oh, trouble," I warned him. "She's
coming this way."

Joey's mom, Mrs. Pignattano, was one of
the shortest ladies I had ever seen, not
counting the Munchkins from *The Wizard of
Oz*. She wore bright red lipstick, an orange
sweatshirt, and bright yellow sweatpants.

"Joey, what's wrong with you?" she
asked. "Why aren't you eating?"

"I hate egg salad," Joey answered.

"Hate?" she repeated. "Don't say that
word. Hate is a bad word. I don't like you
using that word. Never say hate." She
waved a finger in his face.

Joey groaned. "Sorry, Momma."

Mrs. Pignattano messed his hair. "That's
a good boy," she said.

Joey quietly asked, "Can I say that I really, really, really *don't like* egg salad?"

Mrs. Pignattano watched Joey without expression. "Yes, Joey. You can *say* that. But first — eat your sandwich."

Joey moaned, groaned, and took a small bite. He chewed slowly, like it made his teeth hurt. All this, I thought, from a guy who once ate a worm for a dollar. I guess he really, really, really *didn't like* egg salad.

Suddenly, Mrs. Pignattano snapped her head around. She spied a crowd of boys across the room. They were playing catch with Jell-O. Mrs. Pignattano lowered her head and charged down the lane like a bowling ball. The boys scattered fast, like pins after a strike.

Joey didn't pay any attention. He just stared unhappily at his egg salad sandwich. He looked like somebody had drowned his favorite goldfish.

Chapter Ten
The Nose Knows

At long last, it was time for the great volcano show. Ms. Gleason had brought the volcano into the classroom. It almost covered the entire worktable.

Geetha began by explaining that volcanoes were really just holes in the earth's crust. "A long tunnel leads down from the top of a volcano to an underground cave," she said.

Danika Starling stood beside her. She held up a homemade poster that showed the inside of a volcano. "Hot gas from the chamber rises up — and pushes molten rock to the surface," Geetha explained. "The red-hot rock erupts from the volcano and flows down the sides."

Now it was Helen's turn. She walked up to the volcano. "Yuck," Helen complained. "Something smells around here." Helen leaned closer to the volcano. She sniffed. "Has anyone been messing with our volcano?" she asked.

I watched everyone closely. No one said a word. But I did notice Joey Pignattano slump down in his seat. That made me wonder.

"Please go on, Helen," Ms. Gleason said.

Helen held up a small bottle with red liquid. "This is vinegar with red food coloring," Helen said. "The volcano is already filled with a small amount of sodium bi-car . . . bi-carb . . . "

"Bicarbonate," Ms. Gleason said.

"Yeah," Helen said. "What she said."

Helen poured the vinegar into the volcano. In a few seconds, the volcano began to bubble.

And bubble.

And bubble.

Higher and higher and higher.

"Is it supposed to bubble this much?" asked Ms. Gleason. She looked concerned.

Helen shook her head. "I don't think so. I only put in a little."

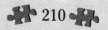 210

"Uh-oh," said Geetha. "I thought it was *my* job to put in the sodium bicarbonate."

"*Your* job?" asked Danika. "I thought I was supposed to do it!"

"Uh-oh, triple bubble trouble!" said Helen, staring at the erupting volcano.

More and more bubbles poured out, faster and faster. And with the bubbles came a horrible smell. I sniffed the air. It smelled familiar. But from where? I looked at Joey — he had his head buried in a book. I saw that it was upside down. Joey wasn't reading. He was hiding.

That's when I knew.

Everyone started holding their noses. Ms. Gleason opened a few windows. Poor Helen looked close to tears. "Why does our volcano stink so bad?" she wondered.

I stood up. "I have a hypothesis," I offered.

"What is it?" Helen asked.

I pulled an index card from my back pocket. I handed it to Helen. It read:

| Need a Mystery Solved? |
| Call Jigsaw Jones |
| or Mila Yeh, |
| Private Eyes! |
| for a Dollar a Day, |
| We Make Problems Go Away!!! |

Helen frowned. "I'm not paying a cent," she said.

Oh, well. It was worth a shot. "Then here's a freebie for you," I said. "It smells like eggs. Actually, it smells like egg salad."

I turned to Joey Pignattano.

Joey looked like he wanted to disappear.

"What did you *do* with that sandwich?" I asked him.

Joey's face turned red. His eyes darted

around the room. He held up his hands. "I hid it in the volcano," Joey admitted.

Everyone waited in silence. We didn't know what would happen next. Would Ms. Gleason be angry?

I heard a soft giggle. Then a snicker. It got louder. Suddenly, Ms. Gleason started laughing out loud. "Bwa-ha-ha!"

Helen laughed, too. Then Geetha and Danika. Soon everybody was laughing — even Joey. That was the end of the stinkiest, and the funniest, science project ever.

School should always be so much fun.

Chapter Eleven

A Salty Solution

Mila and I headed over to Bobby Solofsky's after school. We brought Sally-Ann Simms with us. "You'll enjoy this," I told her. "Just let us do the talking, okay?"

Sally-Ann nodded.

My finger did a few push-ups on the doorbell. The door swung open. I was shocked to see my oldest brother, Billy, standing in the doorway. "What are you doing here?" I asked him.

"Hi, worm," he said. "What are *you* doing here?"

I frowned. I saw a girl standing behind him. It was Bobby's sister, Karla.

Then it dawned on me.

Karla.

Oh, no.

I sniffed the air. Yep, it was Dad's aftershave all right. "Your new girlfriend is Karla . . . *Solofsky*?" I asked.

Billy put his hands in his pockets.

And grinned.

Yeesh.

This was bad news. I tried to figure it out in my head. If Billy fell in love with Karla, they might get married. If they got married, then Bobby Solofsky would be . . . *my relative*!

Double yeesh.

I could feel my stomach doing cartwheels.

I didn't even like *thinking* about it. In fact, I could hardly talk.

"Hey, Bobby," Karla shouted. "Your friends are here!"

Billy put his arm around Karla. "We'll be down in the basement," he said. "Doing homework."

Finally, Bobby appeared at the door. "Hello, *Theodore*," he said. "Mila, Sally-Ann."

Mila nodded hello. Sally-Ann stuck out her tongue. I was still trying to make sense out of what I had just seen. My own brother

— my favorite, all-time best brother in the world — dating Bobby Solofsky's sister.

Triple yeesh.

"Let's get this over with, Bobby," Mila said.

We followed Bobby into his garage. There was a jar filled with water resting on a wooden box. The water was swirling around. As if it had just been stirred. A wooden spoon lay on the box. I touched it. The spoon was wet.

Why would anybody stir plain water?

Beside the jar, there was a bowl with an egg. Bobby slapped eighty-five cents on the box. "That's my end of the bet." He winked at Sally-Ann. "Look familiar? It used to be yours."

Bobby laughed.

Sally-Ann snarled.

"Are you sure you want to do this?" Bobby asked me.

"Sure, I'm sure," I replied.

 219

Bobby mumbled a few magic words, held the egg over the jar, and let it go.

The egg started to sink.

Then stopped.

It floated in the middle of the water. Just like he'd said it would.

"Ha!" Bobby shouted triumphantly. "I win! I win!"

"No, Bobby," I said. "You lose."

Bobby pulled back in surprise. "What are you talking about?"

I quickly snatched the jar from the crate. "Ordinary drinking water, right? That was the bet, wasn't it?"

"Hey, give that back," Bobby protested.

I observed it closely, like a scientist. The water looked a little cloudy. I dipped my finger into the water and tasted it.

Salty, just as I expected.

Mila stepped behind the crate. "Jigsaw, look at this." She reached down and held up a box of salt.

"Cheater," Sally-Ann muttered through gritted teeth. Bobby watched helplessly as Sally-Ann Simms lifted the money off the table.

Sally-Ann tried to give me the money. I refused. "Keep it," I said. "Treat yourself to a Popsicle."

Sally-Ann grinned from ear to ear. It was the first time I'd seen her smile in days.

Bobby just stood there, scowling. "How did you know?" I tilted my head toward Mila. "She figured it out," I said. "With a little help."

"Help?" Bobby asked.

I smiled. "Tell him what your father does for a living, Mila."

"He's a science teacher," Mila said.

That left Bobby speechless. Which was exactly the way I liked him. As we walked away, Bobby called out to me, "I'll get you back one of these days, *Theodore*."

I stopped in my tracks.

I turned and looked at him.

"The name's Jigsaw," I told him. "Jigsaw Jones. Private Eye."

On the way home, Mila started singing. Sally-Ann joined her. Soon they were both hopping on the sidewalk, singing loudly:

"We all bounce on a yellow trampoline, yellow trampoline, yellow trampoline!"

Oh, brother.

Anyway, I was glad. It was another mystery solved. No surprise there. After all, it's what any good scientist would have predicted!

The Case of the
Ghostwriter

Chapter One

A Mysterious Invitation

At four in the afternoon, Mila was doing pushups on my doorbell. I let her in. She handed me a folder. Inside, on top of a few papers, was a handwritten note.

badne	wsth	erei
saspel	lin	gte
stto	mo	rrow
lhopey	oua	refe
eling6	et	ter

I grinned. Mila was always writing messages in secret code. That's because we're detectives. For a dollar a day, we make problems go away.

Mila looked at me and smirked. "Nice pajamas," she observed.

"Don't laugh," I said. "I'm sick."

"I know — you got to stay home from school," Mila said.

My nose was runny. My head ached. My throat hurt and my knees itched. I probably sneezed about three hundred times.

"Ah-choo!"

Make that three hundred *and one* times.

Only two good things happened all day. Number one, my mom let me stay in my pajamas. Number two, I got to rot my brain by watching too much television.

Mila followed me into the kitchen. I poured two glasses of grape juice. "I'll need a minute to solve this," I said.

I recognized the code right away. It was a space code, one of the simplest in the business. The spaces were in the wrong places. I opened my detective journal. I rewrote her message, taking out the spaces between the letters. Then I searched for real words.

Finally, I cracked it. "Rats," I groaned after reading the message. "I forgot about Friday's spelling test."

"And look at this," Mila said. She pulled out a yellow sheet of paper from the folder. It read:

Author's Tea

Come to room 201 and meet a real, live author!

Share books and stories, autographs, refreshments, and classroom tours with a beloved author!

Who is the mystery author?

That would give away the mystery!
(You'll have to come to find out.)

Date: Thursday, May 14th
Time: 9:30 AM
Place: Ms. Gleason's Classroom (201)

 R.S.V.P.

"You're supposed to give it to your parents," Mila said.

"Cool," I said. "I wonder who the mystery author will be."

Suddenly, a loud cry filled the room. "Theodore Andrew Jones! What have you done?!"

Mila's eyes widened.

"You better go." I warned Mila. "It's a bad sign when my mom uses my *middle* name. I'm probably in trouble."

We heard footsteps stomping up the basement stairs. They didn't sound like happy footsteps.

Mila reached for the front door. "What did you do?" she asked.

"Dunno," I said. "Maybe she found my Jell-O city."

"What's a Jell-O city?" Mila asked. Then she quickly raised her hands. "On second thought, forget I asked. I don't want to know the answer!"

I closed the door behind Mila.

She, at least, was safe.

"Theodore Andrew Jones!" my mom yelled. "You've got some explaining to do!"

Chapter Two

Green Wet Slime

Even though I was sick with a cold, my mom made me clean up "the mess" in the basement. I tried to explain to her that it wasn't a *mess*. It was a city made entirely of Jell-O. "It's art," I said.

"It's melting on my rug!" she replied.

My mom sure gets fussy sometimes.

By the next morning it was back to school — sniffles or no sniffles. I felt a little tired. No, I wasn't still sick. I had stayed up too late. That's the problem with good books. I can't stop reading them. And last night, I was reading a real page-turner. It was the latest in the Creep Show series. Number 118, *Green Wet Slime*. I stayed up half the night, reading by flashlight.

I sat next to Mila on the bus. I looked around. It seemed like *everybody* had a Creep Show book. They were easily the most popular books in school. Creep Show started as a book series a long time ago. Then it became a hit TV show. Now

it's *everywhere* — from plastic plates to bedspreads to action figures.

I noticed Eddie Becker talking to Athena Lorenzo. "I'm reading his new one! It's called *Green Wet Slime*! It came out last week."

"I just started reading them," Athena said. "I'm up to number twenty-six, *My Baby-sitter Is a Teenage Zombie from Mars*. It comes with holographic stickers!"

Mila rubbed her eyes. "*Teenage Zombie from Mars*?" she whispered. "Sounds dumb to me."

"No way," I said. "R. V. King writes the creepiest, scariest books going." I pulled *Green Wet Slime* out of my backpack. "I finished this last night. You'll love it."

Mila scrunched up her nose. She took the book with two fingers, as if she were holding a dead mouse. "I'll probably hate it," she grumbled, stuffing the book into her backpack.

School went OK. We climbed ropes in gym. Joey Pignattano got stuck at the top and wouldn't come down. That was interesting. Before dismissal, a lot of kids asked about the mystery author. But Ms. Gleason wouldn't give us a single hint.

"You'll have to wait and see," she said. "But believe me, I think you'll be very pleased!"

Chapter Three

Stringbean

A few days later, I was in my tree house when Stringbean Noonan pulled his bicycle into the driveway. Stringbean's real name was Jasper. He was the skinniest kid in room 201.

"Hey, Stringbean." I waved from the tree house. "I'm up here!"

He looked up nervously.

"Climb on up," I said. I fit another piece into my puzzle. It was a new one based on the *Creep Show* television series. It was

called "Day of the Living Creep." I was almost done.

Stringbean didn't budge. "What if I fall?" he asked.

"You won't fall."

"But what if I *do*?"

I glanced down at Stringbean. I already knew he was afraid of bees, thunder, horses, and lightning. Now I learned he was afraid of heights. "I promise, Stringbean. *You won't fall.*"

Stringbean gritted his teeth. He slowly climbed the tree house ladder. You would have thought he was climbing the Empire State Building. He finally reached the top.

"Whew!" He wiped a hand across his forehead. Stringbean started to talk. I raised my hand.

"Hold the phone," I said. "I just want to finish this puzzle." I had only six pieces left.

Stringbean looked around. "What phone?"

"There's no phone," I said. "I just need another minute of quiet."

"So how can I hold the phone?" he asked.

"It's just an *expression*," I said. "Like 'you're pulling my leg.'"

Stringbean lifted an eyebrow. "I never *touched* your leg!"

"I never *said* you touched my leg," I replied.

"You just did!" Stringbean complained. "You said I was pulling it."

"That's not what I *meant*," I stated.

"Then why'd you *say* it?" Stringbean muttered.

Oh brother. I scratched the back of my neck. "Let's try this again," I said carefully. "I was only using an *expression* — a saying. Do you know what that is?"

Stringbean's face was as blank as a brick wall. I took that as a no.

"Imagine I told you to put the lights out," I said. "Would you take the lightbulbs and actually put them out in the backyard?"

Stringbean laughed. "Of course not. I'd just turn them off."

"Exactly!" I said.

"But . . ."

"No buts, Stringbean," I said. "Besides, what brings you here anyway?"

"My bicycle," he answered.

I sighed. "I mean, *why* are you here?"

Stringbean slid his eyes from side to side. "We need a detective."

"We?" I asked. "Who's *we*?"

"Me, Bigs, Ralphie, Kim, Lucy, and some others," Stringbean said, ticking the names off on his fingers. "They elected me to come and talk to you about it."

"Why'd they pick you?" I asked.

Stringbean fiddled with his shoelaces.

"Well, Bigs Maloney said I *had* to do it." Stringbean looked at me helplessly. "I didn't want to argue with Bigs."

"Good thinking," I said. I pulled out my detective journal. "So what's all this about?"

"The ghost," he replied.

"Oh." I paused. "What ghost, exactly?"

"You know," he said. "The ghost who's coming to our classroom."

Chapter Four

The Ghostwriter

My jaw must have dropped open. Because a second later, a bug flew into my mouth. Yuck, pit-tooey!

"We think the mystery author is a ghost," Stringbean told me. "We want you to find out for sure."

"I get a dollar a day," I told him. "You have the money?"

Stringbean dropped a few objects in front of me. Three pieces of bubble gum. A half-chewed Darth Maul pencil eraser. A rubber band ball. Thirty-six cents. And a Pokémon card, Diglett.

"We were hoping for a trade," Stringbean said.

I frowned. "Everybody has Diglett. Sorry, you'll have to do better."

Stringbean reached into his back pocket. He pulled out another Pokémon card. This one was Gloom. It evolves from Oddish. I looked closer. It was a First Edition.

I snatched up the card. "It's a deal," I said. "Let me get my partner."

I went into my house and got Mila on the phone.

"Now?" she asked. "Can't it wait? I'm in the middle of something."

I said it couldn't wait. We heard Mila coming a few minutes later. Actually, we heard her falling.

OOF! WHACK! THUD!

She tripped over the sprinkler in my backyard.

 245

"Are you OK?" we called down.

"Yeah, yeah," Mila quickly said, rubbing at her elbow. Mila climbed up into the tree house and sat down.

"What happened?" I asked.

Mila held up the book *Green Wet Slime*. "I was at a really exciting part," she explained. "I couldn't stop reading."

We told Stringbean to give us the facts. He said a bunch of kids went to Ralphie Jordan's after school. They were trying to guess the identity of the mystery author. "We came up with only one answer," he said. "R. V. King, author of the Creep Show series.

Stringbean continued, "That's when Earl Bartholemew came by on his skateboard." Earl lived across the street from Ralphie.

"Hold the phone," I said. "Earl Bartholemew is a *teenager*. Believe me, you just can't trust teenagers. Besides," I

added, "I think Earl's a little strange. He's taken too many ramps without a helmet."

Mila spoke up. "Just tell us what happened next."

Stringbean clucked his tongue. "Well, see, Earl's mother is a librarian. She told Earl that R. V. King isn't a real person."

"What is he?" I asked. "A fake person?"

Stringbean leaned forward, eyes wide. "No one has ever seen a picture of R. V. King — *because he's not real*. Earl says he's a *ghostwriter*."

Mila rocked back and forth. "Why do you think this *ghostwriter* is coming to room 201?" she asked.

"You heard Ms. Gleason," Stringbean reminded us. "She said it would be a *wonderful* surprise. We figure she invited R. V. King. But there's a problem. Ms. Gleason invited a ghost — only she doesn't know it yet."

Stringbean left a few minutes later. I drew a picture in my journal of a ghost writing at a desk.

I wrote in my journal:

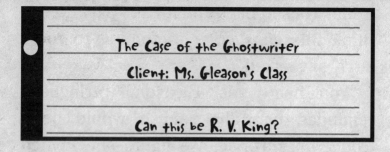

The Case of the Ghostwriter

Client: Ms. Gleason's Class

Can this be R. V. King?

Mila punched me in the arm. "Don't get goofy on me, Jigsaw! Ghosts are *not* real. And they *don't* write books!"

I'll say this for Mila. She's got a pretty good right hand. My arm ached for the rest of the day.

Chapter Five

Family Stories

Ms. Gleason flicked the lights to get our attention. She held up a piece of paper. "Boys and girls, settle down. I'm giving you letters to bring home to your parents. Please put them in your take-home folders."

She gave a stack of letters to Geetha Nair and Mike Radcliffe. They were this week's hander-outers. Ms. Gleason continued, "As you know, we've been reading true family stories in class. We've already read *Abuela* by Arthur Dorros and *The Keeping Quilt* by

Patricia Polacco. These letters explain that we'll soon begin writing stories about our own families. You'll need to find three family stories and write down the information on the recording sheets I've provided. We'll have Buddy Conferences to decide which story to make into a real picture book." Ms. Gleason concluded, "When we're done, every student in room 201 will be a published author and illustrator!"

We all hooted and cheered.

Geetha Nair raised her hand. "Ms. Gleason, I don't think I have any family stories," she said.

"Of course you do, Geetha," Ms. Gleason replied. "Every family has stories."

"How do we find them?" Danika Starling asked.

"Look under the rugs!" joked Ralphie Jordan.

Ms. Gleason rolled her eyes. "Please, Ralphie. Save the jokes for next month's talent show."

Ms. Gleason turned back to Danika. "*Talk* to family members — your parents, grandparents, aunts, uncles, brothers, and sisters. I'm sure you'll discover many wonderful family stories. You've simply got to ask."

That day, we learned about families all over the world. Some were different. Some were the same. Ms. Gleason taught us how to make a family tree. We had to get our parents' help to finish it.

During art, we drew family portraits. I didn't think this was exactly fair. My family went on forever. Three brothers, one sister, Grams, my parents, and a dog — all together in one house! I told the art teacher, Mr. Manus, that I'd need a bigger piece of paper.

He laughed and told me to do the best I

could. I did — but poor Grams and Hillary got squished. There wasn't enough room on the page.

During recess, Bigs came up to me. "Do you really think R. V. King is coming to visit our classroom?"

"Maybe," I said. "Maybe not. I'm still working on it."

Bigs slapped me on the back. It stung so much, I saw spots. "We're counting on you, Jigsaw!" Bigs said.

Mila and I reviewed the case later on. She twirled her hair between her fingers. "You know what we have to do, don't you?" Mila said.

"Yep," I replied. "It's time to see Frank."

Mila nodded. "Frank will know. Frank always knows."

Frank was the owner of Hedgehog Books. He was also friends with our parents. He

knew everything there was to know about books and authors.

Maybe he could help unravel the mystery.

And if that didn't work out, it wouldn't be a total waste. We loved playing with his cat!

Chapter Six

Mila Gets Hooked

I found my parents in the living room. They were playing chess.

"Hi, Mom. Hi, Dad. Who's winning?"

My dad grumbled. "Your mother just took my queen," he complained. "Even after all the nice things I've done for her."

My mom laughed. "What else should I do? Lose to you on purpose?"

"Yes!" my dad answered. "Lose to me on purpose! I love that idea!"

Yeesh. That's my dad for you. A little

goofy. "Um, Mom, Dad? Can you tell me some family stories?"

My dad slid his rook across the board. "Now's *not* a good time, Theodore. I'm trying to destroy your dear mother."

My mom moved her knight. "Check," she said. She tried not to smile. But not hard enough.

"Uh, guys?" I asked. "Remember me? Your youngest son? Do you know any family stories?"

My dad looked up. "Why don't you ask Grams?" he said. "She has some great stories."

Before I had a chance to go find Grams, I heard the doorbell.

My slobbering dog, Rags, raced to the front door. "Quiet down, Rags," I scolded. Rags looked up at me, insulted. I patted his head. "Good watchdog, Rags. Now go back to sleep."

Rags thought that was a great idea.

Mila was at the door. "Hi, Jigsaw! I wanted to return this." She handed me *Green Wet Slime*.

"That was fast. Did you like it?"

Mila lifted her shoulders and let them drop. "My father says it's not real literature. My stepmom says it's junk reading." Mila's face broke into a wide grin. "But I'm totally, totally hooked! Have you got any more?"

I sent Mila away with an armload of Creep Show books. I reminded her before she left, "Don't forget to ask your father for a ride to Hedgehog Books."

Mila smiled. "It's under control. He'll take us tomorrow after school."

That was great news. We needed more clues, fast. The kids in room 201 kept bugging me for answers. *"Who's the mystery author? Who's the mystery author?"*

Yeesh.

Even worse, this family story stuff was getting in the way of my detective work. I doubted Sherlock Holmes ever had problems like mine.

Chapter Seven

My Middle Name

Every night my dad reads to me in bed. He calls it "our special time." Some nights, we don't read. We just lie next to each other in bed, talking about stuff. Tonight, we did both.

He closed the book we were reading. It was *Bunnicula* by Deborah and James Howe. I liked it — the story was funny and spooky. My father yawned and stretched his arms. He leaned on an elbow to kiss me good night.

"Tell me the story about my name again," I asked. "Please."

"Your name?" my father wondered. "Theodore?"

"No, not Theodore," I said. "My middle name . . . *Andrew*."

"Oh." He leaned back down and stared at the ceiling. "Andrew was my brother," he said. "That's why we gave you his name."

"And he died," I said.

"Yes," he said. "Andrew died." I heard the air leave my father's lips. The sound of a deep sigh.

I put my head on his shoulder. "Why did you name me after him?"

My father turned and looked into my eyes. "Because we loved him," he said. "Just like we love you. We wanted to honor him. You should be proud to carry his name."

I didn't really understand. "I never met him, did I?" I asked.

"Not that you'd remember," he said. "We took you to visit him, soon after you were born. Just your mother and me."

"He was sick then?"

My father looked away, then back at me. "Yes," he said, nodding once. "He was very, very sick."

The room was dark and full of silence. We both lay quietly, alone in our thoughts. Not moving. My father remembering. Me just wishing I *could* remember. But I had no memories. My uncle Andrew was just a face in old photographs. Just a name we shared.

My father sat up and swung his feet to the ground. He ran his hand through my hair. "Andrew was very weak and tired," he said. "But even so, he insisted on holding you in his arms. You were just a baby, barely three months old. But you smiled into his face, Theodore. You gave him the most beautiful smile in the world."

That's when I noticed it. The water in his eyes. A single tear, then another, slid down his cheek. My father was crying. I'd never seen him cry before. It made me nervous.

"Don't be sad, Dad." I hugged him with both arms, tight.

He wiped the tears away with the back of his sleeve.

He sniffed hard and smiled.

"I'm not sad, Theodore," he said. "It's just that I remember little things that happened. Little things Andrew said or did. And I'll always miss him."

"Can you tell me?" I asked. "About the little things?"

My father checked his watch. "Not tonight, son. It's late already. But I will tomorrow, promise."

"Good night, Dad," I said. "I'm sorry you're sad."

"Don't be sorry," he said. "That's life, I guess. Sometimes we lose the good ones. Good night, Theodore Andrew Jones. Sleep tight."

Then he shut the door.

Chapter Eight

The Sound of the Creep

Hedgehog Books was a cozy little store. Our parents had been taking Mila and me since we were little. They knew the owner, Frank, and liked him. My mom said that Frank's favorite thing was to bring books and kids *together*.

Mr. Yeh dropped us off at the bookstore. "I'll be back in ten minutes," he said.

Frank was chatting with a customer when we walked in. So Mila and I just grabbed books and sprawled out on the soft, thick carpet. His green-eyed cat, Crisis, rubbed against us to say hello.

When the store emptied, Frank gasped. "Goodness! You kids have to stop eating! If you're not careful, you're going to turn into grown-ups. We don't want that, do we?"

We laughed. Frank was always saying strange, funny things. We told him about the ghostwriter.

Frank listened, rubbing his chin thoughtfully. "I probably shouldn't do this," he said. Then he scribbled on a pad and handed it to me:

R. V. King
555-4440
13 Raven Street

"You can use my phone," Frank said.

"What?!" I said. "You mean — call him? Now?"

Frank laughed. "Go on."

Mila dialed. We pressed our ears against the receiver. A hollow, echoing voice answered the phone. *"Hello, this is R. V. King. I am out rattling chains and walking through walls. Please leave a message at the sound of the creep."*

We slammed down the phone.

"Not home?" Frank asked, smiling. He

snapped his fingers. "I'll tell you what! Raven Street is a short drive from here. If it's all right with your parents, I'll take you there. It will be my special treat. This way, you can ask the author in person. Besides, I'm curious, too." He scratched his head. "I wonder if R. V. King really is a ghost."

"Are you sure about this?" Mila asked.

"Trust me," Frank said. He clapped his hands together. "Now, quick! Call your folks, Jigsaw. We're not going anywhere until your parents give their permission."

My mom thought it was a great idea.

Oh brother.

Mila's father arrived. He spoke quietly with Frank. Then he smiled wide.

We were on our way.

Half an hour later, Frank swung his car down a wide, tree-lined street.

Mila's eyes grew wide. "This is it! Thirteen Raven Street!"

Frank eased the car to a stop. We looked

across a front lawn that went on forever. The house itself wasn't much. It was smaller than the castle at Disney World.

I tried to swallow. But my throat was too dry.

Mila pointed. "If a ghost really *does* live here, he certainly likes plastic flamingos."

She was right. There were lots of pink plastic flamingos — all over the lawn.

Very weird.

Mila hopped out of the car. She put her hands on her hips. "Coming, Jigsaw?"

I looked at Mila, then back at the house.

I got out of the car.

"You'll wait right here?" I asked Frank.

He nodded.

"If you hear any screams . . ."

"I'll come running," he said. "Don't worry, Jigsaw. I'll be right here. *Trust me.*"

Chapter Nine

Serena

Mila pulled on my shirt. "Are you coming or not?" she said. "This is so exciting. We're going to meet R. V. King in person. It's awesome!"

I bit my lip. "Maybe. But what if a ghost really does write the Creep Show books? What if Earl Bartholemew was right? You heard the phone message. What if a ghost really lives here?"

"There's only one way to find out," Mila said. "Follow me, detective."

Yeesh.

Bing-bong-bingity-bong. We rang the doorbell.

A tall man with bushy eyebrows answered the door. He peered down at us from behind a sharp, thin nose.

Mila spoke up. "Um, is this the house of R. V. King? The famous author?"

The man nodded absently.

Suddenly, a woman's voice called out, "Who is it, Cavendish?"

The tall man, Cavendish, turned his head and moaned. "Fans, I suspect."

"Isn't that the bee's knees!" the woman exclaimed. "Well, don't just stand there, Cavendish. Let them in! I so rarely get to meet my readers!"

Mila and I entered a large marble room. A sparkling chandelier hung from the ceiling. Across the room stood a large woman. Her hair was gray and her dress was hot pink. It went nicely with the cockatoo perched on her shoulder.

She held out a hand, smiling. "I'm pleased to meet you. My name is Serena Barnett. But you probably know me by my pen name — R. V. King." Her eyes twinkled with delight.

My eyes raced from her to the cockatoo, to Mila, back to the cockatoo. I noticed that Mila was staring at Serena's feet. I followed her gaze. Serena was wearing a pair of . . . yellow roller skates!

"I think there's been a mistake," I stammered. "We're looking for R. V. King — *the author*."

She nodded, beaming. "That's me! The one and only!"

You could have knocked me down with a wet noodle. "You?" I said. "I thought Mr. King was, er, um, a *mister*."

She roared with laughter. "Oh, pish and tosh! Why do people always assume my books are written by a man? Is it because they're gruesome and scary?"

She winked at Mila. "Did you know that a woman wrote *Frankenstein*? Women can tell scary stories just as well as men, you know. Maybe better!"

She clapped her hands with delight, twirled, and skated into the next room.

Cavendish yawned rather lazily. He gestured with a white-gloved hand.

We followed her into the room.

There didn't seem to be much choice.

Chapter Ten
Very, Very Weird

Serena glided to a beanbag chair and sank into it with a heavy thump. We sat on a couch across from her. The cockatoo remained on Serena's shoulder, nibbling on one of her banana-shaped earrings.

Serena pulled out a large magnifying glass and peered through it. All we could see was her giant eyeball, blinking at us.

Very, very weird.

"Poor dears," she noticed. "You're still confused."

Yes, we sure were.

"Where is R. V. King?" I finally asked.

"Oh, you sweet child!" Serena exclaimed. "There is no R. V. King. Never was. It's just a name I made up!"

"Do you write all the books?" Mila asked.

"Every one," Serena said. "One hundred eighteen and counting."

"I don't get it," Mila said. "Does that make you a ghostwriter?"

Serena chuckled. "A ghostwriter is just an expression. It doesn't mean there's really a ghost involved. It usually refers to someone who writes for a real person without getting credit for the work. They are, in a way, *invisible*. But they aren't ghosts!"

My head started to hurt.

"But what about the phone message?" I asked. "The ghost?"

Serena's eyes twinkled. "Did you like it? I recorded it myself."

"I *still* don't get it," Mila said.

"I'm giving people what they want," Serena explained. "If a fan bothers to call R. V. King, they deserve a creepy thrill. They surely don't want to talk to a batty old gal named Serena Barnett."

I didn't argue.

Serena showed us her "thinking room," where she worked. It was filled to the ceiling with books.

"It's just like Hedgehog," I whispered to Mila.

Serena overheard me. "Yes, it is," she agreed. "I love that bookstore. So cozy."

"Do you know Frank?" I asked.

She hummed softly. But she didn't answer. "I do my writing on the computer," she said. "I don't know *why* I write such ghastly tales. They just pour out of me."

Mila asked Serena where she got her ideas.

"Ideas are everywhere, all around us!"

Serena tapped her head. "And don't forget your imagination. That's where you find the best ideas."

She continued, "It bothers me when people act like writers are special. I'll tell you, there's nothing *special* about me. I just work hard. I'm not any better than a doctor, or a teacher, or a garbage collector. We all have stories inside us. The only difference is that I let mine out."

Cavendish appeared in the doorway. He coughed.

Serena glanced at him, frowned slightly, then rose. "Well, children, it's been a lovely visit. But I must get back to work."

I reached out to shake her hand. But Serena scooped us up into her arms and hugged us tight. "Handshakes are nice. But hugs are better!" She spun us around. "Hugs are what make the world go round!"

Before we knew it, we were outside again. Running across the lawn. Past the

pink flamingos. To the car, where Frank sat reading.

"Everything all right?" he asked.

"Yes," we both said. "Perfect! Amazing! Wonderful! She even gave us autographed books!"

Frank glanced toward the house. He gave a little wave. "Ready to go home?" he asked.

"You knew," I said. "You knew all along."

Frank looked at me in the rearview mirror. He smiled. "Serena and I have been friends for a long time," he said. "I was just having a little fun with you."

I couldn't wait to get home.

I had a story to write.

Chapter Eleven
My Story

My mom volunteered to help make the books for our class. It was her job to type our final stories neatly. No mistakes.

"Are you done yet?" I asked.

"Shhhh."

I paced a few more steps. I stood beside her at the computer. "*Almost* done?" I asked hopefully.

She didn't answer. She just kept tapping away. I liked the sound her nails made when they clicked against the keyboard.

"Done!" she announced. "Let me just print these out."

At last I had it in my hands. My final draft! "Thanks, Mom!" I wrapped my arms around her. "Thanks a lot!"

"Anytime," she said. "I'm proud of you, Theodore. It's an honor to help a real, live author."

A lightbulb went on in my head. "Did you say . . . *real, live author*?"

She looked at me, confused. "Yes, I did. Why do you have that strange look on your face?"

I smiled. "Oh, no reason," I said. "Except I just solved the mystery — thanks to you."

I gave my mom a high five and raced out of the room.

I knew who the mystery author was going to be. I just didn't know if I wanted to spoil Ms. Gleason's secret. But right now, I just wanted to read my story — alone, by

myself. Just me. The pages were crisp and white. They smelled clean and fresh. My story felt . . . *real*.

And I felt like an author.

ANDREW'S BAD DAY

words and pictures by
Theodore Andrew Jones

One day, a long time ago, a boy named Andrew made a big mistake. He got his head stuck between the railings of the stairs and couldn't get it out. I know this is true because my dad told me so. He was there because Andrew was his little brother. My aunt Harriet was his big sister. It was her job to baby-sit because she was the oldest.

Harriet and my dad didn't know what to do. Andrew was crying and crying.

They tried pulling his feet but his head wouldn't move. They tried pushing, but that just made him cry harder.

Finally, my aunt Harriet got a bowl of ice cream and fed Andrew until he stopped crying. Then my dad put on a show with sock puppets. Andrew stopped crying. He laughed and sang. My grandparents finally came home and boy were they surprised! My grandpa got Andrew out by pulling hard on the railings. He was very strong!

Andrew was my uncle. But he died before I got to know him. My dad says that he held me real tight when I was a baby. Now I feel like I know him a little better. I liked this writing project because I liked hearing family stories. I guess it is how we remember the things we don't want to forget. The end!

Chapter Twelve

Surprise!

Bigs Maloney bugged me all week long. He was *dying* to know if a ghost was coming to room 201. I'd just shrug and stare at my feet. Finally, I told everybody that I'd come up empty.

"It might be a ghost, it might not," I told everyone. "I don't know. Even Jigsaw Jones can't solve them all."

I don't think anyone noticed that my fingers were crossed behind my back.

I spied Mila across the room. I slid a finger across my nose. It was our secret

signal. Mila knew, too. Together we had decided not to tell anyone our secret.

Why spoil Ms. Gleason's wonderful surprise?

The author's tea got closer and closer. But Ms. Gleason kept us busy with our family stories. We'd gone from "sloppy copy" to "final draft." Volunteers glued the typed words onto blank pages. Then it was time for the illustrations. We drew them

during writer's workshop. Ms. Gleason told us that the pictures were just as important as the words. Everybody tried to do a great job.

Finally, we handed in our pages to Ms. Gleason. She promised to bind the books that very night. "By tomorrow's party," she announced, "you will all be published authors."

The next day was the author's tea. When we came into class, Ms. Gleason had our bound books displayed on a table. They looked great, just like real books. It was one of the best days of my life. I had a real book in my hands — my book, that I did by myself. Wow.

"You should be very proud of yourselves," Ms. Gleason said. "I know I'm proud of you."

Soon, the visiting grown-ups came into the room. It got pretty crowded. It was funny to see tall Mr. Hiller try to sit in Lucy's little chair.

"When is the mystery author coming?" Helen Zuckerman asked. "I can't wait to meet him."

"Or it," Bigs shouted. He was still hoping to meet a ghost.

Ms. Gleason folded her hands together. She spoke to the parents. "As you know, I promised that we'd get to meet a real, live

author. I realize that some children hoped we'd have a famous author come to our school. I'm sorry, but that's not going to happen."

Everyone sank in their seats, like balloons with the air seeping out. The kids seemed disappointed. But I knew it wouldn't last long.

Ms. Gleason smiled brightly. "Today we have something better! Boys and girls, please stand and face your parents."

"Instead of *one* author," Ms. Gleason said, "I give you a room full of authors. These children, your children, are our real, live authors. Each one of them has written, illustrated, and published his or her own book. Today, we're here to celebrate their work — and their wonderful families!"

All the parents and stepparents, aunts and uncles, grandparents and friends clapped and cheered. We felt proud and happy. We ate cookies and drank apple

juice and gave lots of hugs. During the party, everyone moved through the room, reading the books.

I went up to Ms. Gleason. "Thanks," I told her. "It was a good mystery."

Ms. Gleason smiled. "Why thank you, Theodore. That's quite a compliment, coming from a detective."

It was my turn to smile. "A detective," I said, "*and* a real, live author!"